T0123363

SOLDIER'S SALVATION/ THE GOLDEN BOX

SOLDIER'S SALVATION/ THE GOLDEN BOX

KOA DE'ANGELO

iUniverse®

SOLDIER'S SALVATION/ THE GOLDEN BOX

Front cover design by Steven R. Montello (wonderboy) and Jacob Poole
Illustrations depicted in imagery provided by Jacob Poole Images. Such images are being used for illustrative purposes only. Used by permission Copyright 2020 Jacob poole/poolejac@gmail.com

iUniverse books may be ordered through booksellers or by contacting:

iUniverse
1663 Liberty Drive
Bloomington, IN 47403
www.iuniverse.com
1-800-Authors (1-800-288-4677)

ISBN: 978-1-5320-9698-3 (sc)
ISBN: 978-1-5320-9699-0 (e)

Print information available on the last page.

iUniverse rev. date: 05/04/2020

SPECIAL THANKS

To each and every brother and sister in Christ, through the calling of prison ministry have spent their personal time and effort to bring the Word of God to those that are lost and without hope.

My loving sister Julie who relentlessly applied her editorial abilities and helped guide me every step of the way.

My brother-in-law Steven who meticulously pieced together text and illustrations to fit perfectly as if they were an intricate puzzle to be figured out.

My friend and amazing illustrator Jacob at poolejac@gmail who through his illustrations and images, made my little fable come to life.

Also, to the iUniverse team for their patience, input, and help in seeing me through this project.

Koa De'Angelo

AUTHOR'S ASSESSMENT

As a professional purchaser and traveler, the author Koa has traversed the globe searching for exotic works of art, one-of-a-kind sculptures and many of the most expensive eye-catching examples of unique human creativity.

Koa was very careful not to wander too far outside the path or destination of any venture he chose. Hence, he truly thought he had always known exactly where he was going. Little did he realize that in the material world he had embraced and selected, spiritually he was lost.

Then God entered his life Unexpected.

Soon after, he learned there was a quote from the bible in the Gospel of John verse 15:16 NIV. It read, "You did not choose me but I chose you and appointed you, that you should go and bear fruit and that your fruit should remain. That whatever you ask the Father in my name, He may give to you."

That verse changed his life.

This novel was not only divinely inspired but written in reparation for a novel he had previously penned. That novel was controversial, influential and aimed to lead many astray. This novel is an atonement.

The events, places, and many circumstances described within these pages are accurate and quite possible. Biblical historical fiction has always had a foundation of Truth.

Buckle up and join Koa for a ride into AD 29. He hopes you will enjoy this novel as much as he enjoyed writing it. God bless you.

CONTENTS

SOLDIER'S SALVATION

THE GOLDEN BOX

SOLDIER'S SALVATION

COMMISSIONED TO SERVE

29AD

Crouching low, circling each other like two young lions, their eyes locked, watching each other's every move. In a split second, voicing ferocious growls and moving with great agility and force, they charged, slamming savagely into one another in sheer recklessness.

With determination, they grappled for a few more seconds, then ripped apart from each other, just as the taller of the two men slammed his left fist into the other's solar plexus. With his right fist, he shot an uppercut to his opponent's chin.

The shorter combatant reeled back, roaring with laughter and while rubbing his chin, barked "Is that all you've got? You hit like a girl!"

"Oh yeah? You didn't feel that at all, did you. That's why you staggered around like a drunken sailor there for a second. Listen, big brother, if you want to fight gladiators? You're going to have to step it up a notch."

"I might be a tad shorter than you Anton, but I'm stronger and faster."

"Yeah, yeah, to hear you tell it, I can barely recall the last time we had a good long run together. Now I could be mistaken, but as I remember it you lost.

Grab that old pike over there, the one you found by the lake. You can use the arm shield. I'll use the sword you made from ironwood. Let's see how much power you have left. After a few slaps with this thing you call a sword, we will see who's really in shape."

"Ok Anton, enough chatter. Let's do this."

Just as they start to square off again, Marcus, Anton's brother holds his hand up. "Whoa, hey hold on, wait a second. Do you hear that? So much for our training session, looks like we have company."

Laying down their weapons, they watched as a company of legionnaires, resplendent in their attire of the Imperial Roman army, rode straight for them. The many horses approaching sounded like a slow roll of thunder. The soldiers finally pulled up to them, creating an immense cloud of dust.

Marcus and Anton were not only brothers, having been born one year apart from each other but had always been the best of friends since childhood. Having grown up just outside of the small town of Lazio, about 30 miles from Rome, it wasn't much of a surprise to see the soldiers approaching. The boys only felt a bit curious, as small units of soldiers often patrolled the countryside.

The parents of Marcus and Anton had told their boys more than once that they could pull a few strings with Rome if the two young men really wanted to join the army. After all, to be a legionnaire was considered a privilege. Many men, when they turned of age and being Roman citizens, could volunteer to serve in the Imperial Army of Rome.

As the fine particles of dust cleared, the foremost soldier stopped his magnificent steed not ten paces in front of the boys.

In a commanding voice he bellowed out, "Is one of you, Anton D'Angelo?"

The brother with the piercing ice-blue eyes and longish jet-black hair standing just over 6 feet tall and built like a Greek statue stepped forward. "I am Anton. What do you want?"

"What I want is you. Where is your brother?"

Anton nods to the one standing next to him and says, "This is my older brother Marcus. What do you mean you want me?"

Ignoring Anton's question, the big soldier looks over the man standing next to Anton. Marcus was a few stones heavier but was about as tall and fit as his younger brother. With his long blond leonine mane of hair and eyes the color of dark coffee, he seemed to resemble a Norseman more than a Roman. He certainly did not look like he could be Anton's brother.

With a shake of his head, the Roman soldier said, "I'm sure you wouldn't be lying to me about him being your brother. I am Lucius Atticus, captain of Emperor Tiberius Caesars' Imperial Roman army. It seems your parents used their influence with our army' commissioner in Rome to get you assigned to my company. Apparently, both of you wanted to enlist. Now you have your wish. I would suggest that you gather what you can carry, so we can be on our way."

Marcus blurts out, "Captain! Our parents aren't even home right now. They are at the market. It is not possible to leave without saying goodbye to them."

Just as the captain starts to comment, the two boys notice a disturbance and start to back up as the mounted soldiers who were waiting behind the captain, hastily part to open a pathway. A lone soldier brilliantly attired in the distinctive uniform of a centurion, riding an Arabian stallion, slowly canters up to the front of the group with the air of a royal leader. Without introducing himself, he looks over the two boys and says, "I see my captain has spoken to you. Your parents have favor with our army's commissioner in Rome. The letter they wrote to him explained how fearless and dedicated you boys could be to the Roman Empire."

Marcus casts a sideways look at Anton and mumbles "Oh boy, here we go."

"Have you something to say, boy?" Marcus just shakes his head.

"I am Cornelius Mariona, centurion and commander of one hundred specially trained soldiers. We are one of the elite companies that represent Rome's finest fighting force.

Some of us have been chosen out of the thousands of his emperor's troops to act as personal guards to the emperor himself. Despite what your parents think of you, only after a very vigorous and demanding training session will my captain be the one to decide if you are deemed worthy to be a legionnaire.

If you make the grade, you can look forward to being assigned to personally guard dignitaries and the elite citizens of Rome. You might even get assigned to oversee foreigners in charge of ruling over their own citizens and running territories, whose territories, actually belong to us. Now let's get on with this. I've wasted too much time talking already."

ACQUISITION

The centurion jerks his horse's head to the side, turns slowly and heads back out of sight. The captain, while keeping his horse steady, lifts his arm up and points to a corral made of stone and logs.

Anton saw that he was pointing to the horses that were sequestered on the eastern slope of the family's ranch-style home. The captain looked down at the two brothers and ordered the young men to go and pick out two horses.

Marcus started to protest. "Those horses belong to our parents. We cannot take them without their permission." The captain holds up his hand to silence him.

"It was your parent's request in the first place that brought us here. Do you think your parents expect you to walk back to Rome?"

Anton puts a hand on his brother's shoulder and replies to the captain, "You are right sir. As you say. Just give us a few moments and we'll be ready."

Knowing their mother and father were at the market, Anton looks at Marcus and says, "I'm sure they didn't think they'd be donating two of their prized horses to the Roman army today, they are not going to be pleased, to say the least."

Marcus adds, “This is so unfair, and to think we don’t even get to say goodbye to them. Your right, there is no use trying to argue about it. I’m sure they will understand. I just wish they would have mentioned they had written the letter.”

BASIC TRAINING

Being able to escape the mundane existence they experienced while living with their parents, both Marcus and Anton were quite thrilled to be leaving the town they grew up in.

From the outset, arriving at the training barracks in Rome was an experience they embraced. The mere size of the compound was somewhat overwhelming. One large section of the complex was surrounded by a 10-foot tall stone wall and was the only thing separating them from the barracks and training field of criminals, slaves and even freelance warriors, who were skilled in warfare. Many free men voluntarily signed contracts in the hope of winning glory and prize money. Slave, criminal or free, they were called gladiators.

Although officially, the new army recruits were not to have contact with the men on the other side of the wall. There were times when the two young brothers would catch glimpses of the particularly brutal training sessions by watching the gladiators through the spaces of the entrance gate.

Their own fighting instructions, endurance tests, strengthening sessions, and weaponry training, seemed not so different from what the gladiators on the other side of the wall endured.

Marcus and Anton both relished the intense and precise methods of the specialized legionnaire training and met each trial with great enthusiasm. They had both grown up with a taste for adventure and excitement that couldn't be found while living at home with their parents. The intensity and strict training seemed to have bred even more strength and confidence into the two young men.

They had grown up to be strong and healthy, often competing with each other in all matters of sports and combat. They were always seeing who could lift the heaviest boulders or swim the farthest. They ran races and sparred with old weapons they bargained for or made themselves. Unlike some of the other soldiers that had been in their camp, they were born to be warriors.

When told by the Roman combat instructor to do 1000 push-ups in sets of 100, then 1000 pull-ups in sets of 50, followed by a 3-mile run, while having an 80 lb. pack strapped to their back, both brothers found they could handle the workouts with no problem. What seemed like punishment to others was a typical warm-up to start the day off, before the real training kicked in. The vigorous training sessions were something Anton and Marcus embraced and looked forward to. For few men could best either one of them in the training field.

Both young men took it in stride when their instructors informed them that their training had ended well, they had excelled. Each one of their specialized trainers wished them good luck and said, they were now ready for active duty.

Anton and Marcus now looked at what they would hope to be a grand adventure. After months of drilling, hand to hand combat and special weapons training, they were in excellent shape. Becoming familiar with spears, shields called scutas, swords, pikes, different styles of daggers, dirks, and archery. Their training finally came to an end.

CONFRONTATION AT SEA

During the week of Marcus' 21st birthday, they felt their time had finally arrived. Now, it was their chance to see the world. When they both received orders stating they had been selected to travel across the Mediterranean Sea to a place called Caesarea, they were delighted and ready to leave Rome.

Walking through the harbor, they were surprised by the sheer size of it. Trying to discern which ship was theirs wasn't easy, but they finally figured it out. Not just by the general boarding instructions they had received earlier or the dock number, but 10-meters down the wooden dock-way from where they stood, was an immense and very impressive warship with an Imperial Roman flag flying atop its mast.

"There it is!" Marcus howled to his brother. "Man, that ship is huge, I heard it could hold up to 250 people."

"I certainly can believe that and look at that intricate figurehead carving on top of the bow," responded Anton.

Marcus chimed in, "Look at how they shaped the bottom front of the prow, it looks like a giant rhinoceros horn layered with bronze. I sure wouldn't want that thing ramming into me if I was on another boat."

Boarding the ship dressed in their new uniforms, while lugging their armament along with them, it all seemed very exciting. A dense crowd of people mingling on the dock were laughing, shouting and waving their arms as they gathered to watch the company of soldiers depart.

As Marcus and Anton stood side by side on the deck of their ship, looking all around, they glanced at each other, smiled and simultaneously pounded their fists together and voiced, "Incredible!"

Over 80 slaves, rowing with oversized paddles, cut through the ocean like knives through butter. After what seemed like weeks at sea, many of the soldiers, bored to tears, stood on the bow of the ship daydreaming and letting the calm motion of the gently rolling waves take their minds off to faraway places.

Most of the soldiers including Anton and his brother suddenly heard the faint sound of a roman signal trumpet blaring in the wind. Looking out over the endless sea, Anton spied on what the lookout high above them spotted only seconds beforehand.

He nudged his brother who was standing right next to him and said, "Marcus you see that, out there?"

"Yeah, it looks like two vessels seem to be interlocked and drifting together. Right? Just below the horizon?"

"Yep, I'm seeing it too."

What the captain of the ship realized before anyone else did, was the ship that flew a Joppa merchant flag was under attack. He responded immediately and accordingly.

The captain of our ship hollered loudly for all to hear. "Pirates! Pirates! Those are Assyrian pirates; I know by the shape of their ship. Rowers push forward, make haste, push and pull faster!"

All of our company were on the deck by now. The crew members and the soldiers assigned to escort us had all prepared for situations such as this and were synchronized in what looked to us like a mere scramble.

We literally had to reach out to whatever was stable because our Roman-built one hundred and twenty-five-foot seacraft began to accelerate and within minutes was pushing forward at top speed. Just at that moment, we realized we were headed directly toward the ship that was not displaying a flag. The crazy part was our ship was not slowing down one bit and we were getting closer and closer very quickly.

Our own captain in charge was yelling vehemently for us to hang on tight, be at full alert and ready to board the ship that we were racing towards to intercept. Little did we know that we were not going to stop at all but with full force, we were going to ram the side of the offending ship.

Before we even had the sense to fully prepare for the onslaught, we hit the side of that ship with a thunderous sound like an erupting volcano. A quarter of our company and not a few of the crewmen got slammed to the deck. At once, the ravens, those long boarding planks with 10-Inch nails attached to their ends, crashed down on the other ships deck.

Our ranks immediately started to cross over two by two as six other planks struck the decks of the pirate's ship, like a raven's claws digging into a dove. Since more than half the pirate's crew were now trying to retreat from the merchant ship, we had caught them in the middle. On top of that, their ship was sinking.

The minute my feet touched their deck, four tattered, scurvy looking men tried to rush Marcus and I, who was directly behind me. We had been in this predicament before on dry land.

Three thieves had tried to take us down one night while walking home. We had been partying and had a little too much to drink. Stumbling around, laughing like two drunken idiots, we must have looked like easy marks. It did not fare well for those foolish amateur robbers, as we were not quite as drunk as our assailants had hoped.

As then, the same now, with no hesitation, I swept my sword across the foremost man's chest and went down on one knee to slice the ankle of another, while my brother raised his short bow and fired an arrow into the next man's neck. Drawing the other man's attention by shoving the wounded one toward him, gave me time to catch the last of the four with a sword thrust to his side. The fourth man's momentum, as he stumbled back into a fifth pirate, brought that man crashing into my brother who stood straight up, stepped to the side and let the man fall forward, a short dagger protruding from his chest.

By that time the skirmish on the ship was mostly over, I had figured the outcome. But I was still taken aback, when our captain ordered, "Absolutely no prisoners are to be taken alive."

As I looked around, I saw just how serious he was. I watched him dispose of two wounded pirates without a moment's hesitation.

The merchant ship carried mostly citizens of Rome and Judea. The people were being escorted to Caesarea by a small unit of soldiers. The citizens aboard the ship were hopping up and down, waving their arms, crying and laughing at the same time, just happy about our timely intervention.

The pirate ship was tilting and slowly sinking, our commander, Cornelius, talked with the captain of the merchant ship for a minute, then walked over to the escort officer in charge of his soldiers, patted him on the back and shook his hand. Wishing everyone a safe journey, it was time we all got back to our own ship.

We back tracked across the ravens. A few of our ship's crew stayed to unhook the claws off the pirate ship's decks. When they were done, they dove into the ocean, grabbed the overhanging ropes of our ship and were pulled back up. Some of the soldiers stood on deck and talked about the battle, while others watched the pirate ship silently sink into the depths of the ocean.

What seemed like only a few days later, we heard the sound every one of us was waiting for. We knew our journey was coming to an end.

SOLID GROUND

We snapped to attention, as the loud shouting of the sentinel, posted high above us on the small platform fastened to the ship's center mast, could be heard throughout the vessel.

It was like music to our ears. Land had been spotted. We had made it to Caesarea in less than forty-days. Slipping our giant warship into the crowded harbor was the easy part. Standing around shoulder to shoulder waiting with 90-plus anxious soldiers and an array of crewman to debark, was not pleasant. It was like being caught in a frenzy of pushing, shoving, obnoxiously boisterous giant birds. Each man was intent on being one of the first in line to get off the ship.

Our commander, who had spent most of the entire voyage in his cabin, except when the battle began, emerged onto the deck just long enough to call for order, which calmed most of the men down for just about thirty-seconds. Then the noise level quickly rose again. Finally, the planks were lowered to the harbor's dock and all turned a bit more civil, even though everyone was anxious to feel land again. One could easily be jostled and bumped off into the murky water below if everyone was not very careful.

After disembarking, most of the ship's crew members were off to the street markets, gambling dens and inns of the city. The rest of us gathered a few yards away from the docks, out by the main road leading into town.

JOURNEY TO JERUSALEM

The centurion Cornelius began to convey to us our orders, letting us know he would not be accompanying us the rest of the way. A groan started to rise from our ranks even before he was finished speaking. He had just informed us that we would not be allowed to go into the city of Caesarea.

We were to fall into formation and proceed on foot to the next town which was quite a few miles away and then on to the fort in Jerusalem. His reasoning for such haste was the rumors of rebellion there. He had ordered his captain to quell the disturbance before he arrived.

Marcus turns to Anton, shook his head and said, "And to think we left two of our parent's most valuable horses in Rome. Now we are walking through this desolate and miserable land of hills, dust and sand. I knew we should have gotten in with the calvary instead of getting stuck as common foot soldiers. I'm sure this is not what we had in mind."

Anton looks back at Marcus and quips under his breath, "Would you like some cheese with that whine? Quit squeaking. We are not common foot soldiers my brother, we are legionnaires. Besides, I have heard good things about this region. The women are supposedly very beautiful, and the local food is said to be quite delicious. I've also heard this land is rich with treasure for the taking."

"Yeah, well, it sounds to me like the Jews have sent for us to guard their treasures, not to take it from them."

The march through the countryside was quite uneventful except for the many travelers and pilgrims that were also making their way to Jerusalem.

There were literally hundreds of people on the road, some walking, some pulling carts and wagons, others on horses, donkeys and camels, not to mention more than a few stray dogs and children roaming around. There were even a few chariots traversing the road Rome had built.

NOT SO GREAT ROAD

Had we contemplated exactly what we were getting into, perhaps things would have turned out different. I can't speak for my brother Anton but I'm going to say, I should have thought twice about volunteering for the emperor's army. I am just not loving this trek.

Our uniforms were undoubtedly impressive but arguably a bit heavy. Take the metal and leather helmet, the mostly solid metal breastplate, brass, leather, and wooden shield, sword, spear or bow, and a dagger or dirk, thrown in for good measure. We had quite a ponderous load to carry around. Not to mention the Sargent handing me a small silver trumpet to tote around, just because I opened my mouth while drinking one night and mentioned I had made sounds come out of one. And having to trudge up one hill after another was not my idea of a good time either. The road to Jerusalem was hot and miserable.

"Marcus, are you mumbling to yourself again?"

"Nah, just thinking out loud."

"Okay well, you're the one that said, let's fall all the way to the back of the pack. We've only been on the road for a few hours and already you're lagging."

Marcus looked sideways at his brother and grumbled, "I've got two denarius that says, I'll be leading you by the time we get to Jerusalem."

They finally reached a town. It was not much larger than a village. They had come more than midway to Jerusalem and hoped the journey would be over soon. Just as they arrived at the small outpost, which was attended by citizens when not in use by the army, Marcus yells over at his brother, "Where exactly are we? This can't be Samaria; it seems way too small."

Did you not see the sign on that inn we just walked past? It said, "Warm bath provided. Welcome to Emmaus."

"Marcus, at this point it really doesn't matter where we are, now does it. It's not like we can stop anywhere for a refreshing drink."

The unused military camp was located on the outskirts of the meager town but after walking for so long, the company of soldiers were just happy to receive a meal and a cot to lay their heads on.

As the sun rose early the next morning, feeling rested, the unit had a quick breakfast of tasty bread, fruit, and cheese with a hard-boiled egg or two thrown in, to be washed down with a wooden cup of locally pressed wine. Marcus and Anton, as did a few other soldiers, paid their respects by each giving a few coins to the people who attended them. They were ready to move out.

As they began to line up in columns of twenty, Marcus jabs Anton and says, "Hey look over there!"

They both watched as their captain and three lieutenants rounded the corner, riding four stout looking horses.

Marcus goes on, "I know you weren't going to say a word about that. I don't want to hear about it if you were. Because you know what? Right about now, I'm thinking we made a big mistake not signing up for the calvary."

TREASURE ON THE GROUND

ll was as it should have been, at least for a while, then Marcus points his finger and calls out to Anton, "Hey! What's that?"

"What?"

"That, over there."

"Yeah, what is that? "Let's go take a look."

Marcus snaps, "Breaking formation isn't one of your best ideas, little brother. So, if we're going to do this? Hurry up, let's do it fast."

As they rush over and come closer to the pile of vivid colored material lying between the bushes, they hear a meowing sound like some kind of trapped animal and then the bundle begins to stir. The brothers both take a step back.

Marcus yaps, "Whoa, what in Hades?" Just then, a piercing, ear-splitting squeal erupts from the pile.

Anton bends down and lightly touches the heap of dull colored fabric with the tip of his sword, looks up at Marcus and whispers mostly to himself, "Oh, no."

Marcus blurts out, "Don't even say it"

"Sorry, but yeah, it's a child."

"So now what are we going to do?"

Anton looks at Marcus and shrugs "What you're going to do is unstrap that little thing you've been carrying around on your shoulder and give warning.

Marcus cringes, "This is for emergency purposes only."

"Marcus, someone left a child on the ground, in the bushes, like so much trash for the animals, the vultures and anything else that would eat it. Do you not think this is an emergency?"

With that, Marcus raises the small instrument to his lips and blows a warning note from the small silver trumpet. Immediately the column of soldiers that had kept marching up the road, came to an abrupt halt. A few seconds later, the entire unit turned, reversed and started to jog back to where the brothers were standing. Within about a minute and a half, the captain was standing directly in front of them and was not looking very happy about the delay.

"You sounded the alarm! I don't see any trouble here. I'm going to presume this wasn't a test of some sort."

Anton stutters, "No, it wasn't sir. This is the trouble, sir." Then, he extends his arms out in front of him showing the captain the small baby. The leader's eyes go wide but in a second they return to normal. He says nothing.

Anton continues to explain while pointing to the bushes off to the side of the road, that the child was left over there to die.

"We spotted the brightly colored blanket in the bushes, had no idea what it was, then heard the cries. What could we do?"

The captain gives the two soldiers an annoyed look and retorts."

Without any hesitation, the captain tells them, "You could have kept marching and not broke rank."

With an almost undetectable grin, the Sargent says, you found the child, it is your responsibility. What I want, is for both of you to get back in line and continue marching. At the first dwelling, we come to, you will go up to the house and say to the occupants, by the order of the Imperial Roman army they are to attend to the baby until further notice. After all, the child is presumably a Roman citizen. I will make a report when we get to Jerusalem. Just make sure you catch up quickly when you're done. "No more lagging."

After falling back in line and moving on down the road with the rest of the unit, Marcus quips, "Another fine kettle of fish you got us into, brother."

Anton only smiles and says, "Yeah right. Who's the one that spotted him first? Anyway, I'm the one carrying him. Stop complaining, you'll wake him up."

"Him? How do you know it's him?"

"I peeked. The blankets were all wet."

"Well brother, we could be in luck. Look what I just spotted over there."

After a couple of hard knocks on the fragile wooden door, it slowly opens to reveal a time-worn middle-aged bearded man and a pleasant-looking woman standing just behind him.

With a kindly but firm voice, the man asks, "How can I help you today kind sirs?"

Marcus speaks up, "Are you the proprietor of this property?"

The man answers, "Yes, I am Jacob, and this is my wife Andrea. I own a small vineyard out back. Can we offer you two a cup of wine?"

The two soldiers just stare at the man. "Ok then, how can we be of service to two of Rome's finest soldiers?"

Marcus snorts, "I don't know about that but-"

Right then, the baby Anton is holding makes a musical sounding sigh.

At once, the woman nudges her man aside, steps forward and says, "Oh my, and what do we have here?"

Anton takes a step toward the woman and presents the little bundle. She reaches out and takes hold of it. Without a word, holding the baby in both hands, the woman slowly sinks to her knees, pressing the child to her bosom. Suddenly she bursts into tears and starts to sob uncontrollably.

As she kneels at Anton's feet, her husband Jacob reaches out and puts his hand on her shoulder, and sighed, "I'm very sorry, for you see, our child of eight months old, died only two weeks ago."

Staring at the scene before him, Marcus was absolutely speechless. Anton is able to explain just how they came upon the male child and how their captain ordered them to find a home for the baby. He goes on to tell them a report has been made out. It will be filed in Jerusalem when the soldiers get there and will be promptly lost in the shuffle, as this child is of no importance to Rome or anyone else. "Basically, the child is yours now."

At that moment, the woman calms down. She then rises up and stares into Anton's eyes.

"Through you, by the grace of God, this child has been delivered to us."

Marcus breaks the spell as he asks, "And what god do you speak of, woman?"

Andrea looks at Marcus. "My friend, do you know what a divine appointment is? It is no accident that you two were guided here today. There always was and always will be only one true God, the Creator of our universe and that is Yahweh.

It is said, "The Son of Man now walks this land doing great wonders and is called the Christ Jesus."

Jacob adds, "Thank you, my friends. Through you, our God has delivered a miracle to us and we shall call our son Stephen.

With the child in good hands, the brothers bid the new parents farewell and jog off down the road to catch up with their company.

Rome had done quite a magnificent job carving out and paving their roads throughout the empire. This one leading into Jerusalem, they named it the Great Road.

JERUSALEM

The legionnaires arrived in Jerusalem just in time for the Festival of Harvest, apparently a very important Jewish holiday. It seemed all Judea's citizens of the region were in a high spirited and joyful mood. Anton and Marcus, along with the rest of their unit had settled down into a very imposing barracks. The sort that neither one of them had ever been in before. The massive stone structure was called the Antonia Fortress. It looked more like an old castle.

The building itself was quite impressive. It housed over four hundred soldiers at any one time. In the barracks itself, there was a multitude of small windowless rooms. Each area was supplied with three comfortable looking cots. Cups, bowls and spoons, were neatly laid upon the tops of folded blankets.

Looking over his shoulder at Anton, Marcus snickers, "Very impressive, this is what I'm talking about. It actually looks quite comfortable."

Anton grins, "they did say that this place is reserved for the most elite legionnaires and brother, that would be us."

The Antonia Fortress was separated by a deep wide trench, across from a magnificently built temple that rivaled anything they had ever seen in Rome.

Early the next morning the entire company, consisting of soldiers who had made the journey together from Rome and at least 40 others that had come in from other companies were called into formation. Each one was granted a six-hour pass so they could become familiar with their surroundings.

A NEW FRIEND

Raffa, who was about the same age as the two brothers, had already been at the fortress for about three months when they met on the training field. Marcus, always proud of how strong he was, became more impressed with his new friend's strength as time passed. One day while training together, Raffa, being just about the same size as Marcus, lifted up a 350lb rock and military-pressed it over his head, not once, not twice but three times. Marcus, being quite competitive tried lifting the same rock but could barely haul the big stone up to his chest. Anton, rather wisely, gave Raffa a nod of respect and declined to even bother trying to lift the big boulder.

This day, Raffa decided that he would give the two brothers a little guided tour and walk them through the markets and squares of the city, for it seemed like the whole place was enjoying the festivities.

As they passed the various vendor booths and stalls that lined up on each side of some of the streets, not for the first time, they overheard snippets of conversations describing a new teacher, perhaps even a real prophet, who some said, was claiming to be the Messiah.

Upon hearing the rumors for the third time, Anton turns to Raffa and says, "What are those people all talking about? Why are they getting so excited about someone like that?"

Raffa just utters, "I'm not really sure. I think it's some kind of new religious idea that a man is promoting and some of the Jews around here aren't too happy about it."

The hours passed quickly as they examined rugs from Persia, sculptures from Greece, paintings from Syria. They sampled delicacies baked out of small stone portable ovens and looked at the different styles of clothing for sale. Even stopping for a few minutes to watch a slave trader describe the benefits and delights of the three young girls he was offering.

Anton just shook his head and snapped, "I don't care if the sex trade is lawful or not, I think it is disgusting.

Sometimes I just wonder why people treat each other so harshly."

Marcus leans over and whispers, "Hey little brother, slow your roll. Your sounding like our mother every time father brought up the subject of buying a slave for the house."

"Whatever, sometimes the things people do to each other is just not right."

THE ARMORY

After a long day, by the time the two soldiers returned to the barracks they had just enough time to go to the canteen before it closed, get something to eat and call it a night. Right before getting to their bunk area, Raffa caught them walking down the long hallway.

He walked up to them and said, "Hey fellas, you're not trying to go to bed already are you? You do know because of our legion status; we don't have a curfew like the Auxilia soldiers do."

Marcus groaned, "Well, I am kind of tired."

Raffa retorted, "Come on wuss, you can sleep when you're dead."

Anton kind of perked up and said, "Raffa what did you have in mind?"

He then told the boys his uncle was the Master of Arms. He oversaw the fortress armory. Raffa said, he had been invited to visit him a while back but hadn't had a chance to see him yet. He thought tonight was a good time and wanted to know if they would like to come along.

Now, Marcus was getting enthused, "You can get us into the armory? How wild would that be? I've heard they work all day and all night. They create all sorts of weapons. Raffa, good looking out, yeah, I really do want to go. Anton?"

With no hesitation, Anton answers, "Yep I'm in."

Ten minutes later just down the road from the barracks, the three young soldiers arrived at what looked from the outside like an immense dark storage unit, then just a few seconds later, they heard a relentless muffled hammering sound, Like that of a giant heartbeat.

Raffa said, "This must be it, that noise has to be coming from inside and besides there is nothing else around here."

Raffa started pounding on an oversized dark metal door. From the inside, the door sounded like it was being unbolted and began to slide on some kind of a roller. Just then an enormous sized man that covered most of the entrance stepped out.

He must have been at least six-five and looked to weigh about four hundred pounds of solid muscle. His hair was not the style of a typical Roman soldier but fell to his shoulders. He was clean-shaven and had a surprisingly pleasant looking face, although his eyes were another matter altogether, they were a deep gray with tiny speaks of gold in them and were quite penetrating. They seemed to pierce right through as he looked at you.

"Nephew, is that you? Are these your friends? Everyone needs a few good friends around them. You never know when somebody will try to stab you in the back. Come in, come in, let me show you what I've been working on."

As we passed through the huge door, we saw that the vast space was a lot bigger than it looked from the outside. It could have passed for a large cavern. The only light that shone came from a few strategically placed very large candles, some pitch torches that hung from the sides of the walls and five fired up blacksmith stations that looked to be in full service.

It was all very intense, very noisy. With men of all sizes manning the billows in front of the kilns, while others fed thick rods of iron into the hot furnaces. All the while, more sweat-drenched men stood in front of the furnaces, pounding relentlessly with over-sized iron sludge hammers, smoothing, shaping and straightening the brilliantly red glowing metal.

The room itself was not only dark and cast shadows everywhere, but it was also very hot, very uncomfortable. It didn't seem to bother the men that were working there one bit as they joked and hollered good-natured obscenities at each other.

Raffa's uncle, whose name was Gallo, reached over to a small table and picked up a very sharp-looking oversized spearhead. He made it clear to the three young men standing before him, that he had personally designed and oversaw the making of the spear's point. He let them know he had made the spearhead for a well-known centurion, who was also a very good friend of his. Gallo held it out to show them the details of his work. He explained to them, it was made with bronze instead of iron. It was lighter but just as strong as iron. He was sure his friend would be pleased with it.

As he was talking to the three young soldiers and pointing out the different types of weapons that were being made for the armory, he led them over to a crude-looking wooden table covered by a large dark piece of leather.

The big man suddenly stopped and said, "You're going to like this. Come close, I don't want anyone else to see this. Step a little closer."

With a flick of his wrist, he snatched the leather covering off the table.

Marcus literally flew back and crashed into Anton as Raffa tried to get out of the way. "Whoa, What the-what is that?"

Gallo raises his head back and roars with laughter. Barely containing himself he howls, "That was good, that was really good. I like you boys."

As the young men quickly recover from their shock, they realized the black thing on the table wasn't moving. For there lying on the table, dark as night, coiled up like a large evil-looking snake, was a good-sized thick pitch-black colored whip. Inserted into the pommel were two ruby red stones that reflected off the dim candlelight, shining brightly, resembling viper eyes.

After getting himself under control, Gallo grins at the three young men staring at him and says, "The difference between a flogging whip and a scourging whip is this, while a flogging whip is shorter and made from strips of leather, this scourging whip was made from dried leather strips of treated oxen hide and then dyed black. The strips are at least five to six feet long and not only have marble-size steel balls tightly braided into the last six inches of the strips but also have the dismembered claws of raptors and sharp shards of bone woven into the tips of the whip."

He begins to explain, "When the whip strikes flesh, the metal balls will cause deep bruises which will then break open the skin. With further strikes, the shards of bone at the ends of the whip will begin to lacerate and shred the neck, shoulders, oftentimes even the sides of the face.

A whip this long can reach all the way down the back to the buttocks and legs. This will leave bone fractures, internal bleeding, massive tearing, and will turn ones body into raw ribbons of bleeding flesh. Sometimes the sufferer's veins are laid bare and the very muscles and sinew of the victim are completely open to exposure."

Quite diabolically, Gallo turns and with a big innocent looking smile stares at the men standing in front of him and boasts, "My captain has forbidden me to wield the scourging whip anymore because most of the men that I've ever served it to... did not survive long enough to be crucified."

The three men, standing stock-still just shake their heads, all in a bit of a shock as the last of Gallo's words began to sink in.

Raffa says to his uncle, "It is getting quite late and we must be getting back to the barracks. Thank you, uncle. That was quite a tour and will not be easily forgotten."

"No worries boys, it was my pleasure and you are welcome here anytime."

As the three young soldiers start to retreat out of the big metal doorway, Gallo calls out to them, "You are all looking quite fit, if the inclination ever comes to you to leave the legionnaires, I can see to getting you reassigned to the armory."

As they walk away, Anton lowers his head and quietly whispers to Raffa, "You do know that your uncle is completely insane. I'm thinking, this is the last place I'd want to be assigned to."

Raffa nods his head and says, "Yeah he is a little over the top, a little extreme."

Marcus looks over, "Extreme? That's not quite the word I'd use.

Anyway, Raffa thanks for asking us along. It was quite interesting, to say the least."

FIRST ENCOUNTER

The next day, Anton and Marcus, along with ten other soldiers, were assigned to patrol the north side of the city. As they came to an intersection, the officer-in-charge commanded them to walk the perimeter of a large park located just down the road, when they were finished, they would return to the barracks.

The officer complained it was a very hot day and there was really nothing going on anyway. Everyone seemed to be good with that, so there was nothing more to be said. As they patrolled along the edge of the park, they came upon what seemed to be a good-sized area containing a garden bursting with beautiful flowers and shrubbery. Walking further on they saw a variety of colorful orchids, hibiscus, and roses clustered around a few large boulders.

Drawing closer to the interior of the park, Marcus stopped and said, "Hey look, there are people gathered over there."

They proceeded to skirt the park's flora and understood the mass of people they had spotted on the other side of the boulders was a much larger crowd then they had first suspected. They were all standing together listening to someone speaking.

Seeing a few of the Pharisees present, Marcus quietly said to the soldier in charge, no one is paying any attention to us. Let a couple of us go over near those trees where we won't be so conspicuous. We'll be able to hear what's going on. The one in command pointed to Anton, Raffa along with Marcus and signaled them to move closer to the trees.

As they stood not twenty feet behind the crowd, they heard the one that was speaking.

"I have told others at the temple; having heard the words I spoke; they are not my words but are my Father's words. And for those who have witnessed or heard of the works I have done, I tell you now, those works I did, I did in my Father's name. I boast not. For my Father is in me and I am in my Father."

Then from the side of the crowd, a Pharisee yells out to him, "Is not your father Joseph the carpenter?"

At just that moment, a woman and her young daughter started to move through the crowd toward the front, where the man was speaking. As they nudge by a small group of Pharisees, one of them holds up his hand and cries out in a sour tone to the woman, "Move back, this is no place for a woman and a young child to be."

With downcast eyes, the woman softly responds, "Pardon me, kind sir. My daughter only wanted to come closer so that she might see more clearly the one who is speaking. Because of an affliction since birth, she cannot speak, and she is also very hard of hearing."

As the woman was explaining this to the Pharisee, the man that was speaking to the crowd walked up to them. He politely asked the Pharisee to step aside. He then knelt on one knee in front of the little girl, gently put his hands on her shoulders, tilted his head and whispered into her ear. A few seconds later he then stood up and walked away. The obnoxious acting Pharisee looked right at the child and demanded in a loud voice to tell him what the man said to her.

The little girl smiled, and as she looked up at him said, "Sir, you do not have to yell at me, I can hear you now."

He said to me, "I am glad you came to see me and listen to me speak even though you could not hear me very well, for you are a child of God... do not forget me."

Upon hearing her daughter speak, her mother fell to her knees and hugged her daughter passionately. With tears of excitement and immense joy, she looked up at all the people that had been standing near and cried out, "My daughter is six years old and has never spoken a word since birth ... until now. Praise God! That man healed my baby girl. He is a true prophet and more than a prophet. He is the Anointed One."

The people all around them become deathly quiet and then all at once started to stir, looking all around for the one who had spoken to the little girl. Not seeing him anywhere, they began murmuring and pointing toward the woman and child.

Anton turned to Marcus and Raffa asking them, "What just happened? What did you see?"

The crowd at that point was starting to get a bit unruly. Thirty paces away, two of the Pharisees were in a heated argument with a small group of men.

At first, no one noticed the three soldiers standing just behind them until Anton took the shoulder of a young man, turned him around and asked, "Who was the man speaking?"

The citizen said, "He is the one called Jesus."

Just then, the rest of the soldiers who had stayed in the background started to move forward. The soldier in charge yells into the crowd, disperse and go about your business. The show is over. Go and enjoy the park. As the crowd scattered, the three soldiers start to move back the way they came.

Later, while lying on his bunk, Anton questions himself. "Why do I think of him? What is this feeling that urges me to want to hear more of his words?"

The next day, while talking to Marcus, Anton mentions the little girl and her mother.

"I'm still not entirely sure what happened out there but truly, I have never seen two people instantaneously become as joyful as that woman and her daughter."

Marcus replies, "I know exactly what you mean. The craziest thing is, I thought I heard the voice of Jesus somewhere before. I felt at peace for the moment."

Raffa, who was standing near, watching and waiting for them to finish talking, so they could go to breakfast said, "What is the matter with you two, are you going soft on the Jews?"

POLICING THE TEMPLE

Early one morning, while lying around on their cots inside the barracks, waiting for orders and wondering what the day may bring, Anton and Marcus heard their names called out as the captain read off part of the roll call and told all the soldiers, whose names he called to report outside to the front of their barracks.

Still a bit sleepy, as they made it to the fortress' courtyard, both brothers perked up as the captain said, "The sixty men I've called, have been chosen as a special unit of Roman legionnaires. You are under my command. This man standing next to me is the honored centurion Cornelius DeMariona whom some of you may remember from your voyage here. You will now listen closely as he explains your orders.

Looking quite impressive, the tall soldier in his scarlet and brightly polished metal centurions' uniform, stepped forward. With a clear commanding voice, that all could hear, he sternly proclaimed, "Your job will be to oversee the Jewish temple guards. For all intended purposes, you are going to be keeping a close eye on the Sanhedrin, which is part of the Jewish Highest Court of Justice that also intertwines with the Supreme Court of Jewish Council. The Pharisees, Sadducees, scribes and especially the high priests, entertain the falsehood that they can maintain their territories and citizens, without the help of Rome. They are deeply mistaken.

You will fall under the direct command of the Jewish Council outwardly. In reality, you will be reporting to your captain their every move." The Antonia Fortress is now your permanent home until such time as you may be transferred to another section of our great empire."

Anton quietly turns to Marcus, "Looks like we're not going to get to fight gladiators or lead men to war for a while."

Marcus shakes his head, "Looks like we're now working for the Jews. I guess it could always be worse."

Their assignments stayed the same except now they all took their orders directly from a Jewish high priest named Joseph Ben Caiaphas. On one of their first assignments, the high priest Caiaphas called sixty of them to an assembly in the courtyard of the temple.

He walked out of the temple's entrance looking like an emperor, in a long tunic of royal blue, tied with a golden sash. His long skirt's waistband was trimmed with tassels. Small golden bells hung from his hem, tinkled as he walked. He wore a second tunic over the first garment. It had much fine gold and hand embroidery woven into it, over that, was a very thin breastplate of gold and silver inlaid with twelve shining gems that made a circle.

There were two larger precious stones set in the middle of his breastplate that was rumored to be ancient and magical. Some scribe had told a soldier, the two large stones placed there had the special names of Urim and Thummim and were a direct link to their God.

Our captain had mentioned to us earlier he believed the stones had absolutely no power whatsoever and how utterly ridiculous the Pharisees looked, strutting around in their brightly colored costumes like peacocks, thinking their laws were greater than Caesar's laws. We now saw what our captain was talking about.

Caiaphas, explained to the detachment, "He was a man of peace, a man of God."

He said, "There were dissidents about, and they were bringing unrest to his people."

He stated, "That these men were blasphemers, rogues, rebels and thieves.

He complained, more and more, his voice raising in pitch "The common citizens of Jerusalem were starting to listen to a newly-arrived false prophet."

Caiaphas gripped on about how more than a few had even started to follow the one they called Jesus.

He said, "He knew for a fact that this man was just a lowly carpenter from the town of Nazareth."

He then heatedly shouted, "This man has the audacity to claim to be the Messiah. He even has the nerve to suggest he is the Son of God.

I want you to patrol our fine city. The streets, parks, and markets, wherever.

I want you to disperse any crowds or groups of people that you come upon listening to public speakers.

If perchance, you come upon the one called Jesus? He needs to be immediately arrested and brought directly to me any time, day or night. Is that clear? Is that completely understood?

My own temple guards are under the same orders as you, so make no mistake, he will be found and he will be brought to justice, just as any other rebel would be."

Later that evening, while in the fortress, both Anton and Marcus started hearing different rumors about those who followed Jesus, stirring up their own people, while wandering in the streets of Jerusalem.

Raffa over supper said, “He heard Jesus had actually raised a young child from the dead and he and some of his disciples were now preaching in the town of Bethany, not far from here.

This man has become a bit infamous since the first time we laid eyes upon him. Perhaps we need to find him and have a chat with him.

MEAN STREETS

Dawn had come quickly. Anton and his company were assigned the task of not only walking the perimeter of the praetorium and temple but were also to patrol some of the inner streets of the city.

Raffa, who had gotten promoted to Sergeant, was in charge of a small unit now and decided to take only eight of us and let the other twelve that were assigned to him, stay on the grounds of the fortress. All seemed peaceful as we proceeded down the narrow lanes of the town but as with many things in life, in a blink of an eye, it all changed.

As the soldiers turned the corner, they spied, what looked like a small skirmish taking place about thirty yards away. Breaking into a fast-paced jog, Marcus, yelled out to the group of three or four men fighting, "Stand down! Stay where you are."

Upon hearing the soldiers running towards them, the assailants stopped kicking, what looked from a distance, a man lying on the street. The men turned and fled in two different directions, leaving the man lying in a fetal position on the dirt road.

Anton bent down and put his hand on the fallen man's shoulder. "Hey, are you okay? Are you hurt?"

The man slowly shook his head, turns his face toward Anton and said, "Thank you, sir. Those men were of Arab descent and must have spent the night drinking or something. When they saw me coming toward them, they started laughing and calling me names, taunting me, disrespecting me because I'm Jewish. It was in my nature to correct them, to tell them now I follow the Way. I started to share the good news of Jesus with them. When out of nowhere one of them blindsided me. That was pretty much it, I'm no coward but there were four drunken fools on me, so I pretty much just folded. I fell to the ground, tucked up like a turtle and prayed. Father God answered my prayers by sending you to me."`

As Anton reached out his hand to help the man stand up, he asked, "What is your name?"

"My name is Bartholomew. I thank you again and may God bless you. I truly believe this was a divine appointment. I believe we will meet again."

"It's funny you should say that. Not so long ago a woman said that very same thing to me, as I handed her a child that we found on the road that had been disregarded like so much garbage."

As Bartholomew dusted himself off, he looked around at all the men and said, "May God be with all you soldiers and may his angels guard your way."

As the man started to walk away, Marcus called out to him. "And what god do you speak of?"

The man stops, slowly turns around and speaks in a clear and gentle voice. "His Son walks among us and will be revealed to you in his time."

Even though Marcus seemed to remember hearing that same answer somewhere before, he looked at his fellow soldiers, and grumbled,

"What kind of an answer was that? Angels? And whose son? What was he talking about?"

The other soldiers stood there looking perplexed.

Anton shrugs. "I have no clue. I don't know about his god, but I do know we arrived right on time to stop him from getting a real beating.

FAIR OF WONDER'S

The days were passing by quite quickly. Whoever coined the phrase, "Never a dull moment" had it right as far as our company was concerned. Every day and night when the soldiers checked back into the barracks, there were always the day's adventures to be heard and stories of past exploits to be told. Jerusalem was not a dull place to be stationed.

Being assigned to the Pharisees was not quite as boring as it first sounded. It seemed the high priest and his cohorts had only one priority that weighed on their minds, it was the ongoing disturbance to the population in general, caused by whom they referred to as the rebels. This not only included those Jewish dissidents that violently opposed roman rule but also any and all Jews who did not adhere to the strict rules of the Sanhedrin.

Today, like on most other days, our company would split up into three columns. Each patrolling a separate area of the city.

Raffa, who was our sergeant in charge, told the twenty of us gathered around him, he heard there was a pretty good size fair going on at the south end of town. He said, "It might be a good idea to check it out." We all agreed. Who could pass up a festivity? Especially while on duty.

As our unit of soldiers drew near the designated area, one could hear the merriment going on long before we got there. The fair was hosted on a large plot of land and was fenced off to make it look more official.

As we entered through the gate, a plethora of sounds and colors burst upon us. It looked more like a large gypsy camp than a fair. So different from the Roman fairs or markets back home, even the first marketplace we went through when we first arrived in Jerusalem was of no comparison.

There were musicians playing flutes, horns, drums, and an array of different style string instruments. The combination brought forth a captivating effect, as somehow the different tones, all blended creating an upbeat joyful sound that drifted throughout the fair. The air was adrift with the smells of exotic and tantalizing food, mingling with the scent of people and animals.

Raffa decided it would be a good idea to split our column in two. Ten men taking one side and ten walking the other side. He told everyone to be back at the front gate in thirty minutes.

The venders yelled from they're wooden kiosks. Some of them only had flimsy make-shift stands and booths, while others put up small open tents, held up by wooden poles, even a few sat or stood to present their goods to be sold. There were flowers, jewelry, sculptures and paintings, toys made of wood and other materials for the young ones and at every turn, clothing and trinkets hung from the stalls, imported from various parts of the country. We saw handmade candles, hats, backpacks, and displays of different kinds of stones, some precious, others, not so much.

There was even one man selling hand-made weaponry, such as bows, swords, daggers, maces and custom-made metal gloves. In one corner of the fair, there were pony rides for the children and even a petting zoo with an array of small animals, waiting to be fed by those that came to look.

Hawkers walked around the fairgrounds, intermingling with the patrons, yelling out their wares, selling an assortment of treats for the children. Others sold small bits of questionable food on small thin sticks or in brightly colored wrappers.

Many vendors offered a vast variety of different styles of food. It seemed there was food offered not only by the people of this territory but by people from many other parts of the country as well. Everywhere we looked, everything was for purchase. There were even fortune tellers beside bone and card readers. We also saw the silhouette of one supposed clairvoyant and seer mysteriously hidden behind a thinly veiled enclosure. Yes, the assignment of patrolling areas of the city, was not so tough... yet.

RIVER MAN

Today was not much different from the rest, but hey, at least it wasn't raining. I'm thinking, Raffa loves overseeing our unit, better him than me. I'm speaking for my brother Marcus also. We were just content on serving the best we could without having to take on a lot of responsibility for others. At least formally.

Oh, we all did look out for one another. That was a given. The longer we served together the more we came to know each other. Our unit became close, almost like a family.

If there really was rebellion going on? It seemed weak for the most part. We keep getting reports of small skirmishes, but we hadn't run into much of anything like that yet.

"Hey Anton, are you daydreaming again?"

"Nah, just picking up one of your bad habits. Talking to myself. Why what's up?"

"Raffa wants us to fall into formation. We've got five minutes."

The first thing out of Raffa's mouth as he walked up to us was, "You two should have been with me last night. I'll have to tell you all about it later."

He turned to the rest of his men and spoke, "Right now, we're going for a bit of a walk. We're taking off to the outskirts of the south end of the city. We are going to check out a report of some suspicious activity happening down by the waterway. I think it is a reservoir that branches off from the Jordan. But don't quote me, all I know is that our orders are to patrol the area."

With that being said, they started to move out. Just about forty minutes into their march, one of the soldiers cried out, "Hey! Look over there, that is a lot of water."

Another soldier quips, "It sure looks inviting."

Someone else asks, "It's moving, is it a small river?"

Another chirps in, "It could be what some locals called the spring of Gihon, but I think it's a reservoir. I don't really know the difference."

An instant later, Raffa barks, "What in Hades is going on over there? See, over there? Where those people are standing in the water."

Pointing his finger, he stammers, "Look further out. It looks like there's a man trying to drown someone out there. "See? Look, look, the other man is splashing around, he just dunked him in, looks like he's holding him underwater by the neck!"

Raffa and Marcus both unsheathe their swords, and began to run towards the riverbank. The rest of the soldiers see the commotion now and start to follow.

Wading in the water, Marcus starts for the man who moments ago held the second man under the water. The man lifts the other's head and shoulders up out of the water and embraces him. The man, that seconds ago had been submerged beneath the water, looks ecstatic and is practically glowing with joyfulness. He lifts his hands to the sky and moves toward the small crowd as they start applauding and began to sing praises.

The first man still standing in the water, starts to move slowly toward the soldiers. He looked to be fit and was quite tall in stature. He was not much older than any one of the soldiers that had entered the water. He pressed toward them. His demeanor looked quite fierce, all wild hair and beard, penetrating eyes, and dressed in an array of what had to be wet animal hides. As his stern-face broke into a kind smile, he spoke in a clear voice. "My cousin, why do you seek him?"

Raffa responds, "Your cousin? who is your cousin? We thought something was amiss here. We were rushing over to see if everything was all right. We had at first thought that you were harming that man."

"Oh, I am sorry. Have you not heard of baptism by water? I thought it was my cousin you were looking for."

"Riverman, perhaps you are mistaken. We were assigned by the emperor himself to oversee the temple guards here in Jerusalem. We also watch, we patrol, we look for thieves, robbers, and rebels, who not only cause trouble among your own people but also cause unrest and turmoil against Rome itself. We are in this district for your benefit, for your safety and protection."

"I am protected by the one true God. I have no need for man's protection."

Marcus scoffs, "Huh, you say that now but watch yourself, even one who stands in a river dunking people in the water cannot always foresee trouble, sometimes it comes unexpectedly. These are troubling times, my friend. Because of this so-called rebellion that seems to be stirring up the people around here, just beware."

"My name is John of Essenes. I have come a far way from the desert of the east for one reason only and that is to pave the way for the lamb of God. I baptize those who come to me to repent for their sins. I baptize those who wish to change their lives and walk in sin no more. It is a baptism of water. Now the time has come that one walks among mankind that baptizes in the Spirit.

God created the universe, the world and everything in it. Just look around you. He created everything that is visible so that we may begin to understand the invisible. The existence of this planet means there exists another far greater kingdom, that is perfect and awaits those that seek it.

And yes, kind sirs, I will tell you all the truth, if you are a believer of the Way, nothing is to be unexpected. Because, all things, all circumstances, and all life itself comes through the will of God."

After bidding the strange man in the water goodbye, the soldiers walk away from the bank of the reservoir. Anton looks back and sees' the one called john already leading a young woman by the hand into the water.

Heading back to where some of their fellow comrades are standing, Raffa decides to have everyone start heading back towards town, for soon it will be dusk.

MORE THAN A SKIRMISH

They had gone only a quarter of a mile or so up the road when they all heard what sounded like yelling and screaming in the distance.

Raffa bellows out, "Now what?" And immediately shouts to his men to fall in. "Make your weapons ready!"

With shields by their sides, lance's upright and swords drawn, they start to jog in unison towards the disturbance.

As we ran, I began to contemplate our situation. My brother Marcus was the fearless one, not only in his appearance but also his recklessness belied his Roman heritage. If he wasn't my true brother, even I might think he had Viking blood in him. He always thought he was infallible.

I sometimes worried a bit, always being the practical one. I kept thinking, we really haven't seen that much action since arriving at the Antonia Fortress. I just wonder, what did we really sign up for, what is in store for us? Even though there is the talk of an ongoing rebellion, the city, seemed peaceful enough, that was until we turned the corner.

First, we saw women and a few children running straight toward us. For a second, it looked like they were going to attack us, but they quickly veered to the right and got out of our way. While rushing past us, one woman turned toward us and started yelling and pointing back with her finger, but we could not understand her. Perhaps fifty yards ahead we could see men fighting with each other at the end of a cul-de-sac.

There were small houses, more like huts, on each side of a wide dirt road ending with three slightly larger buildings. Perhaps the buildings were being used for storage or livestock.

This was the Palestinian section of town, and we noticed from earlier patrols, some of the people that lived nearby, were not that friendly. So naturally, we had to be on our toes. There were twenty-two of us that made up our unit. We all felt very confident. Why wouldn't we be?

It looked like an easy putdown. Just another small skirmish. We'd gotten well down the street by now and were just starting to close the gap when a fellow legionnaire howled and fell to the dirt, sword, and scuta gone askew. I glanced over at him to see an arrow sticking out of his leg.

Immediately Raffa roared, "Gather close men. Align your scutas now.

I want ten men in front, ten scutas up top. Tortoise formation."

At once we planted our scutas down on the ground. While the others brought theirs overhead and tilted them slightly inward. In unison, we each sank to one knee.

"Titus, shield Lucius with your scuta and see to his wound," Raffa commanded. Then yelled, "Five stay forward, five reverse, to cover our backs. And the rest of you hold up your scutas so no projectiles can get to us from above."

While huddling beneath their partner's shields, the ones carrying bows and arrows began to search out their targets. Not so hard to figure out where the attacker's arrows were coming from, as the gang of rebels were by no means professionals and were making mistakes.

The Roman sharpshooters did not miss. Their arrows flying true, time after time. In less than five minutes, no one was shooting at us from the rooftops anymore.

Raffa commanded those in back, to reverse back to the front with the rest of us and form columns of four. Marcus was ordered to sound the alarm. As he blew a piercingly loud blast from his trumpet, Raffa, then called for the testudo formation. Standing side-by-side with our scutas fixed so closely together we formed an unbroken wall, a solid surface without any gaps between them, our unit advanced toward the end of the cul-de-sac and then began to run forward.

There were only eight or nine men standing before us. They had apparently faked the brawl. Now they all faced us, with weapons drawn. At that moment, out of nowhere, coming from all directions, more rebels began to run at full speed towards us.

The collision of men, the crash of scutas and weapons was deafening. The rebels, screaming obscenities at us, while trying to do battle with an array of inferior weapons was just crazy. Some of their swords snapped off at the hilt upon contact with our superior made weapons. A few of their handmade shields burst into pieces, as they slammed in contact with our swords and scutas made of Roman bronze and ironwood.

After dispatching an unusually large rebel, I stood rooted in place for a second, looking around for my brother Marcus, just as a boy of no more than sixteen ran up and tried to bean me with a makeshift mace. As he lifted his feeble looking club for a second strike, he suddenly stood stock-still and with a look of complete bewilderment on his face, he keeled over right in front of me...With an arrow sticking out of his back. I glanced around but I had no idea where that shot had come from.

Where was my brother? The whole foray had lasted for what seemed like an hour. It lasted only about ten to fifteen minutes, If that.

After patting another Soldier on the back, Marcus stepped out of the mix. Two men lay unmoving in the dirt near him. With a wide grin on his face. He shouted, "Brother, you look so serious, so solemn, not to worry. I had my eye on you. I had your back whether you knew it or not. I saw you take down that big one over there. I'm not sure whose arrow it was that hit the kid but I had you covered. It seems our backup arrived just in time to scoop up the remainder of the rebels.

Anton looked around, "There were others close enough to hear our call?"

"Yes, apparently part of company six was just four blocks away, they even captured one of the leaders. Goes by the name of Barabbas. It was said, he was wanted for murder and the robbery of his own people. What a piece of work he must be. Talking the young ones into robbing and terrorizing unprotected people to support his cause of revenge and retaliation for what he said, we Romans did to his family and friends. For sure brother, he will be crucified for his deeds. You can bet on that."

Anton looks at the ground, "So much for me thinking that this was a peaceful town. Marcus, I'm just glad you're ok. We did lose a few good men today and for what?"

Marcus responded, "Cicero told me, he talked to one of the soldiers from the company that came to help us out. He said that the rebels spotted us down by the waterway and that they had been spying out our route. They staged a fake rumble, in order to trap us between the houses. They even made the women that were there, run out into the street to grab our attention. They threatened to kill the children if they did not do exactly what they were told. It was never going to work out well for them. In fact, we have eight injured and two dead. It didn't really work out so well for any of us."

INQUIRING MINDS

Starting their new day's walkabout, Anton looked around and said, to no one in particular. "This is turning out to be a beautiful day."

As the soldiers passed a temple gate, lying around in a semicircle on the grass out front was about seven or eight people having a quiet discussion. The soldiers, thinking nothing of it continued on their way.

Marcus and Anton, as usual, were walking and talking, bringing up the back of their column. They happened to pass by the small group, just as one man got a little excited and said, "Jesus seemed to know exactly who I was, and I had never met him before that day."

Anton tugs on Marcus' arm. "Hey, wait a second. Slow down. I want to talk to those people we just passed over there."

Marcus calls out to Raffa and motions for him and the men go on ahead. "Anton just wants to check something out. We'll catch up in a minute."

Raffa gives him a thumbs up. By the time Marcus has walked over, Anton was already bent down next to the man who had been speaking and was asking him his name.

The man looks at Anton and says, "My name is James, and this is my brother John."

He makes a hand gesture, "These kind people are our friends. How can I help you?"

Marcus looked down at the man, "We need no help from you but as we passed by we overheard one of you speak the name of the one we seek."

James, with a benevolent look on his face, asks, "And whom might that be?"

Anton begins to stand up, and says, "You know quite well who we mean."

James looks up at Anton and quietly mutters, "Many seem to be seeking him these days."

Marcus retorts, "We have orders. Directly from the High Priest to arrest this man when we find him. In fact, we could arrest you and your brother right now if we wanted to, just for talking about him to these people."

James looks first at his brother John and then looks up directly into Anton's eyes and says, "But you won't arrest us, will you."

As he looks at Anton, he continues speaking. "I see in your eyes; you are curious and want to know more about the Messiah. I will tell you both, as I close my eyes, I can still see him... as if my eyes were open. I feel in my heart and know in my soul that he is always near."

Anton shakes his head, feeling a bit off. A bit mesmerized, not nauseous but maybe just a little unsteady.

He nods to the brothers still sitting on the grass and says, "James, John, what we want you to do, is get up and walk away. All of you. Go find something else to do or somewhere else to talk."

As both Anton and Marcus leave to catch up to their troop, Marcus asks, "What was that all about? Are you okay? You went a little pale there for a second."

"Yeah, I'm good. I Just had a strange feeling there for a second.

The man James was right. I do want to know more about this one called Jesus."

It soon became more than mere curiosity that pushed the two young soldiers to investigate as to what sort of man Jesus was. Not only when the two soldiers were on duty but even on their own time, they both started to consciously listen to people, to see if they might hear where this Jesus might be speaking or even perhaps, healing someone. It seemed whenever they arrived at a spot where someone had told them Jesus might be, they seemed to always be one step behind and would just miss him.

NOT SUCH A HOLIDAY SEASON

As the days passed by, nothing much out of the ordinary occurred. A few domestic squabbles on the poorer side of town, a couple of vendors fighting over kiosk space in the marketplace, a few burglaries, some robberies but for the most part nothing came up that wasn't manageable. Then, just a few days later, things started to change.

It was only a few weeks or so before another of the many Jewish holiday feasts would start. Many people from other parts of the region and beyond, had begun to trickle into the city. It was the day after Sabbath, and everyone seemed to be in a festive mood. The citizens of Jerusalem were joyfully shopping, running errands, picking out decorations and basically gearing up to celebrate Passover.

Standing aside a ways from the crowd, while being entertained by watching the action of the citizens running about through-out the day, Raffa's detail was just about to call it a day and return to the Antonia Fortress and let the night patrol take over, when suddenly out of the crowd, a Pharisee quickly approached them. Getting within hearing distance, with an authoritative voice, he cried out, "Where in the name of God have you all been?"

The lot of us just looked at him with disdain. Raffa blurts out "Where have you been?"

The Pharisee did not seem to take notice of the retort and continued to cry out, "Not an hour ago, the one you were supposed to be watching for, the same man who has been causing all the trouble throughout the territory, blatantly rode down the main road, not three miles from here, on a donkey no less.

He was being praised by hundreds of people. They were waving flowers, palm fronds and even laying some of their garments on the ground in front of him for his donkey to step on.

They had no shame, as they openly blasphemed. Shouting, Jesus, he is the Messiah! He is our King! He is the Anointed One. Can you believe that? It was disgusting to hear. And not a soldier in sight. What are you good for?"

Anton just shrugged his shoulders. Raffa steps forward and in a voice that neither Marcus nor Anton had heard before, for it was the voice of a true commander. He literally hollered into the Pharisee's face, "Stand back priest! Do not ever speak to my men, nor to me in that manner of tone again. We are legionnaires of the Emperor's Imperial Roman army. We are not children, not someone any of you fools can order around whenever it pleases you.

If I ever hear such insolence come out of your mouth again, you are going to have a very big problem. Priest or no priest, is that understood? What, nothing to say? The west-side of this city, it's not our responsibility. Go cry to the 6th regiment, not us."

The Pharisee, completely stunned for a second, made a sour pickle face and screamed, "Am I not a man of God? A man of goodwill and peace? I am an esteemed member of the Sanhedrin and I will not be disrespected or talked down to by the likes of you. You will be reported, and your superiors will hear of this."

The outraged Pharisee, then turned and hastily merged back into the flowing crowd. The soldiers were tired and thought no more of it. At least until that evening.

Walking back into the barracks that night, Marcus, Raffa, and Anton chanced to pass a small huddle of temple guards, when Marcus overheard one of the Jewish guards speak of the man, Jesus.

He called out to his brother and Raffa who were walking just ahead of him, "Hey hold up for a sec."

Just then, they heard the guard say to his comrades, "We got a complaint earlier today. This man named Jesus was apparently causing problems at our temple. They say, "he went a bit insane. Smashing things, screaming insults, tipping over the money changers tables and unlocking the caged birds and animals. Apparently, he made quite a mess of the courtyard"

Someone else said, "I was told he had some kind of whip made of cord and was slapping people around with it. With our luck, at any moment we will probably be ordered to go back out and arrest him. Another guard pipes in, "I thought the legionnaires, the council brought in, were supposed to be handling things like that. Come to think of it, the name Jesus is already on the High Priest's list of suspected rebels and criminals."

Anton barked, "Marcus, Raffa come on, leave it be, let's walk. We're Romans and we are doing our job. It's not our problem if the Jew guards talking about him have no clue what's going on. We should probably just stay out of it."

As they proceeded to the barracks, Marcus says to no one in particular, "I have a strange feeling we have not heard the end of this and as far as staying out of it? We'll see how long that lasts."

No more was said about it, but later that night, Anton felt a little anxious. He thought to himself, who really was this person that has come to dwell in my mind and has the attention of the people. Anton had seen him up close, heard the words he had spoken and knew Jesus emulated only peace and goodwill as he shared his gospel with others.

THE BETRAYAL

It must have been four or five nights later, in a deep sleep, Anton dreams of a lion standing alone on a hillside, watching a small herd of sheep. The lion started to move down the slope of the hill, toward the flock. Anton is rudely awakened by the sound of his captain's voice, yelling for everyone to rise.

"Get dressed, I want everybody outside now."

Marcus calls from across the room, "Hey, what time is it?"

From a dark corner, Raffa utters, "What? I have no idea. We have no windows in here. I know it's late."

As they all hop up and assemble outside in the courtyard, the captain shouts out, "We have just had a report that the one we have been looking for, the one called Jesus, is not far from here. Our orders are to go and pick him up now. Three Pharisees will accompany us to make sure this is the one they want."

In a quiet tone, Anton whispers over to Marcus, "This is just great. We must lose sleep, get up and go out in the middle of the night, grab someone that has done nothing wrong far as we know and it's taking how many of us to do this? Ridiculous."

It took the soldiers twenty or so minutes of continuous jogging to get close to the place where the informant said he would be. One of the soldier's remarks, "It is quite dark out here. How are we ever going to find him? We don't even know what he looks like."

The captain overhears the man and said, "We are going to the Mount of Olives, it is not that far now. It has been told to us, Jesus and some of his followers will be there, near a ravine just inside the garden gate."

Some of the soldiers look back and even though it is quite late, realize that a good-sized group of people has been following them, in anticipation of what might be going to happen.

Raffa says, to no one in particular, "Doesn't anyone sleep in this town?"

Right then, a man steps out of the shadows and waves the Pharisees over. We barely overhear him as he said, "Come over here. I will show you who you are looking for."

Raffa, turns to the crowd of onlookers and shouts, "If you're so curious and want to see anything? Have one of my men help light up some of those sticks you have brought along but stay out of our way."

The soldiers, Pharisees, a few scribes and most of the pack, entered the garden together. At that point, most of the soldiers had slowed up, some had even hung back and not entered the garden.

Halfway into the garden, they see a small group of men sitting by a torch, stuck in the ground. As they came near, one man stands up. Immediately the man that had met the soldiers at the entrance of the garden hurries over to him, holds him by the shoulders and kisses him on the cheek. He then stumbles back and fades into the night.

By now, all who had been sitting, begin to rise. The one that was already standing takes a few steps toward the soldiers and asks, "Whom are you seeking?"

The captain answers, "Jesus of Nazareth."

The man replies, "I am He."

That very next instant, the soldiers and all who stood near them, immediately fell to the ground. Quickly recovering and standing back up again, the captain looking a bit dazed as he glanced around at his men, dusted himself off and said, "In the name of all the gods, what just happened?"

"In a voice, little more than a whisper, Jesus answered, "What happened was, there is only one true God... my Father."

Just as three soldiers and a Pharisee laid hands on Jesus, a man cloaked and wearing a caul, stepped up to Jesus' side and with the quickness, drew his sword and sliced off the ear of one of the Pharisee's servants. With a mere flick of his hand, Jesus touches the man's ear and says, "Be well, you have not been harmed."

Everything happened so fast, the soldiers knew not what to think, as the servant looked none the worst. Both Anton and Marcus stood to the side and just stared as other soldiers grabbed Jesus and bound his hands behind him. When they looked around for the others that were with him, they saw that his apostles and friends had all scattered. Jesus being alone now, the soldiers pushed him forward and shuffled him away.

WALKABOUT

With Jesus secured and already being led out of the garden, Anton began to replay in his mind all that he had witnessed. He turned to his older brother and whispered, "Man, I don't know about you, but I was standing right there in front. I saw the servant's blood jet out of the side of his head… And then I didn't. The next moment there was not a drop of blood anywhere to be seen. How was that possible?

Marcus, trying to keep a brisk pace and talk at the same time grumbles, "Exactly and what about getting knocked on our asses? It felt like I hit a brick wall. Then, like a flash of lightning, I could see nothing. No pain, no sound, just nothing. I had no idea what happened. One second I'm standing next to you and the next moment we are picking ourselves up off the ground, all twenty or thirty of us. Seemed whoever was standing next to us or even around us, ended up in the grass."

Anton agrees, "I don't even remember falling. Very strange my brother, very strange. Where is he?"

Marcus just points up ahead, "Towards the front."

Someone said, "We are taking him to a priest's house."

Anton replied, "House? Not the temple?"

"I don't know. I guess not."

By the time the two young soldiers entered the courtyard, the yelling and taunting had already begun. The soldiers and Pharisees had Jesus pinned at the back of the terrace.

Anton could hear the old priest bellowing to the soldiers about waking him up. Saying, “If Jesus was demanding a real trial? Go and take him to my son-in-law’s, and if he’s not? Take him there anyway. My son-in-law Caiaphas is the one in charge now. He’s the one worried about all this and wanted him so quickly found in the first place and now you have him. That is where the soldiers should have taken him, not coming here and depriving me of my sleep and wasting everybody’s time.”

It was early in the morning, getting close to sunrise, most everyone was getting tired. To hear Raffa tell it, apparently, we were all going to have to turn around and head back to the temple, which was right next to the Antonia Fortress. We were to bring Jesus to Caiaphas the high priest. He was the one that pretty much had us on call ever since we got stationed at the fortress.

When everyone finally got back through the gate of the temple, Caiaphas, having already been informed that we were on our way, was standing on the front steps... Impatiently waiting.

TRIALS AND MORE TRIALS

The captain hollered out, "If I called your name, you are dismissed. Go back to the fortress and await further orders." He then turned and took Jesus up the steps.

Anton, walking with Marcus looks around and says, "I didn't hear our names being called. So I guess we're stuck here for a while. Hey, look over there someone has started a small pit-fire. It's cold, let's go over there and get warmed up."

While they stood around waiting, watching those on the steps talking, they overheard one of the high priest's servant's say to one of the men standing near the fire, "Are you not one of his disciples?"

Taken aback for a second, the man replied, "I am not."

A few minutes later, one of the other soldiers standing with them said to the man, "You kind of look like one of them that was in the garden earlier."

"You are mistaken, I do not know him."

Marcus chimed in, "You're telling us, you weren't in the garden earlier?"

The man looked at him. "I don't know what you're talking about."

He then turned and walked away. Far off in the distance, a rooster crows.

Anton, glancing over at the stone steps of the temple, sees two soldiers holding Jesus, leading him back down the steps with his hands still tied behind his back. It looked like he hadn't fared too well, as his face looked very bruised.

Raffa called out, "Fall in, we are going to the Praetorium."

Marcus grumbles to Anton, "At least we're headed back toward the fortress."

For the Praetorium was not far from the Antonia Fortress.

Anton surmises, "apparently, Caiaphas needed the governor to hold a trial in order to convict Jesus of a major crime. Word has it, Jewish law forbids Jews from putting any of their own to death and it looks like that is desperately what the high priest Caiaphas wants to do with Jesus...Kill him.

So off they went, escorting Jesus to Pontius Pilate the governor of Judea. Raffa's men and one other small detail were all that was left of their unit as most of the other soldiers had been dismissed. Even their captain didn't seem to be close by.

Anton slipped his way up close to Jesus as they walked. He nodded to him, got his attention and offered him water from the flask that he carried. Jesus just looked at him. Anton would later declare that Jesus had given him a warm smile.

Just as Anton was about to lift the flask to Jesus' mouth, the captain came out of nowhere and yelled, "No water! Fall back soldier, let the prisoner be."

Anton stepped back as some of the other soldiers passed on by.

By then Marcus had caught up to him. "Not such a good idea huh? What were you thinking?" Anton didn't bother answering.

It was early morning when they finally made it to the Praetorium. As the soldiers walked Jesus toward the entrance, the large door of the building opened up. Standing tall, was Pontius Pilate, governor of Judea, which included the district of Jerusalem.

The high priest Joseph Caiaphas, who had accompanied the soldiers, shouted out at the governor, "This is the man! The man, I have spoken to you about time and time again. The one who is causing all the trouble.

We have brought him to you so you can pass judgment on him."

Pilate, who had just stepped out of the door said, "Priest, bring him right in and we will settle this matter now."

Caiaphas took two steps forward then stopped in his tracks, hesitated for a second then groaned, "Sir, our custom forbids me to enter at this time."

Hoping not to have to give any explanation and possibly insult the governor, he stayed quiet.

Pilate stands there for a second then said, "As you wish."

He listens to the high priest, followed by a couple of enthusiastic witnesses with too many accusations. All of them ringing false.

Pilate turns to Jesus and quietly said, "What do you have to say for yourself? What do you think about all this?"

With a serene look on his face, Jesus just shrugs his shoulders and says, "Everything is as it should be."

Pilate looks over at him and utters, "What is that supposed to mean?" Jesus looks at the ground and says no more.

Pilate orders Raffa and two other soldiers to bring Jesus inside as the rest of us veer off to the side along with the Pharisees. Pilate leads Jesus through the door, for a bit of privacy. Within fifteen minutes, here comes Pilate back out the door, followed by Jesus in the clutches of two soldiers and Raffa bringing up the rear. Pilate looks at the priest and then out at the courtyard. Which is now teaming with people.

"This man has done nothing wrong as far as Roman law is concerned."

As he walked down a few more steps and faces the High Priest, he snapped, "It is just about sunrise, I have had no breakfast and I might not even be fully awake yet. I find no fault with this man. What is your deal bringing him here so early in the morning?"

Caiaphas is livid. Barely able to contain himself, he demands Jesus' life. He growled at Pilate, about how Jesus has broken numerous Jewish laws.

Pilate is beside himself, remembering what his wife had told him about Jesus. She hadn't even wanted to come to this year's Passover and complained to him about having strange dreams ever since she arrived here. He silently wished he was back in Caesarea. "I will not pronounce this man guilty of anything.

Pilate, then asked Caiaphas, "Do you say he is from Galilee? If that is so, King Herod is visiting Jerusalem this week for the festivities, he is not far from here. I will send this man to him and see what he has to say about this matter. Perhaps he will see it your way, but other than that? I am done with you."

Pilate calls the captain over to let him know that he wants him to take Jesus to where King Herod is residing. He turns to the high priest and tells him that he may accompany the soldiers also if he'd like.

Then Pilate said, "Come back and let me know what the outcome is. I'd like to know what our esteemed king thinks about this mess you've created."

Caiaphas stares daggers at Pilate, starts to walk away, turns back and snarls, "Be as rude as you'd like Governor, but we'll see who has their way in the end."

Raffa puts Anton in charge and directs eight other soldiers including Marcus, to stay back and try to clear out some of the crowd that has gathered in the courtyard. Anton embraces the responsibility if only out of frustration, collects his men, just as the rest of their unit take Jesus away.

Anton, Marcus and the other seven soldiers' herd most of the people out of the immediate area. The Praetorium being quite near to the temple and Antonia Fortress, there were still a lot of soldiers and citizens milling about even though it was still quite early at that point.

It must have been mid-morning, as Anton and his tired eight-man crew walked the perimeter of the Praetorium.

As he glanced over at the entrance, he saw that most of his unit was walking back in, led by Caiaphas and three other priests. No one looked very happy. In fact, a few of the soldiers looked quite distressed, the others just looked exhausted.

Walking slowly in the middle of the pack, was the man Anton immediately distinguished from the others. Jesus walked with his hands still tied behind his back. Then came a multitude of shouting, boisterous people. Many more than just those that had followed the soldiers throughout the night into the early morning.

Anton thought this whole facade was not only ludicrous but was getting very serious. He decided to take his men through the throng of people to see if he was needed. Once again, the high priest Caiaphas walked back up the stairs.

Out comes Pilate, looking bitter. "Back so soon? What is it now, priest?"

A couple of soldiers push Jesus forward with the help of two other Pharisees as Caiaphas says, "King Herod demands that you handle this business of ours. Do not try and wash your hands of this. This is your district. Your city. The Sanhedrin must have justice."

"Alright then, you want justice. For what? I do not know. What really is the truth? One of your customs does say, I could legally release someone to you at Passover."

Pilate then turns around on the steps and raises both of his hands high above his head. The ever-increasing crowd that had gathered in the courtyard of the Praetorium, abruptly becomes silent. Pilate shouts out at them.

"Should I release to you, the king of the Jews? For this man has committed no crime under the Imperial Roman law. I say, he has done no wrong."

Many Pharisees, scribes and Sadducees had strategically placed themselves amongst the people that had gathered there. With very little prompting, people began to cry out in loud voices, "No! Not that man. Crucify him! Crucify him! Release the one called Barabbas he belongs to us. This one is a blasphemer, a false prophet, an evil magician and a rebel."

Marcus standing to the side with the rest of their company, looked over at Anton in astonishment and exclaims, "Brother? Do you know who they're talking about? They are talking about wanting to release that fool we arrested a few months ago that tried to kill us. They're talking about letting him go. What's up with that? Unbelievable."

Insanity thinks Pilate. He reaches up with his hand and rubs the back of his head. He reasons, perhaps if he punished Jesus harshly enough, that would appease these idiots. A captain of the 3rd-regiment is standing nearby, glaring at what was quickly turning into a vast mob of people.

Pilate hollers over to him "Have your soldiers take Jesus over to the fortress courtyard. Take him to the flogging post and deal with him."

The captain, in turn, calls to his sergeant and tells him to handle this. The sergeant, quite tired of the whole ordeal and not really wanting to bother with any of it, waves Raffa over. Even though they are both sergeants but because he has seniority, he asks Raffa, if he would get six of his men and take Jesus to the pillar and make an example out of him.

He tells Raffa, those Jews want him dead. If he did this for him, he would owe him one. "Have one of your men go find your uncle Gallo. He will make short work of this and we will be done with it."

SHEDDING BLOOD

Raffa commands two of his soldiers to hold Jesus where they stand and not to move. He tells them he will return in just a few minutes. He then trots over to the other side of the building to find Anton, Marcus and a few others in deep conversation. He interrupts the group and steps closer to Anton.

He lets him know that he is now in charge of seeing that Jesus is well punished. "The crazy part is, they want me to find my uncle and not just have him flogged but to scourge him, possibly to kill him."

"You have met my uncle. If he wields that scourging whip he's made, he will kill him."

Anton runs both hands through his hair, then takes Raffa by the elbow and walks him a few paces away from the rest of the group.

With a forlorn look, he sighs and softly said to him, "I have seen this man up close. I have looked into his eyes. This man is innocent. He has done no wrong. He has harmed no one and he deserves none of this."

"Raffa, not only have we been roommates for a while, fought side by side but we have become good friends. I am now going to ask you a big favor, a special favor. You might think I'm cracked but bear with me. Just hear me out before you decide.

Your uncle will not kill him, because you cannot find him. I want you to let me be the one to deliver the thirty-nine lashes to Jesus.

We were all trained in the use of the whip, just like everything else. This burden is mine to bear. I want him to survive." Reluctantly Raffa agrees.

As they arrive with Jesus to the courtyard of the fortress, people start to push and shove each other, while others rushed up, trying to latch on to Jesus. These people should not even have been allowed into the courtyard. The soldiers just shrug their shoulders and look on in disregard. There are people hanging out just outside the gate, while others stand clogging the entrance of the gate itself.

People tried to hit Jesus with their fists and sticks. Others try slapping, spitting or throwing stones and garbage at him.

Some even grab at his beard and pull tufts of his hair out. What made things even worse, was some of the soldiers that were only supposed to be walking him to the flogging post were laughingly striking him in the face and slapping at his legs with their swords as he stumbled along.

As things seem to escalate and get more hectic, many more soldiers from the fortress were being assigned as crowd control. It now looked like some kind of grand festivity was in progress.

The men lead Jesus to the whipping pillar. Raffa looked around, spotting a soldier, he commanded him to run to the armory and fetch the implement needed.

Two soldiers shove Jesus to his knees and tie his hands above his head, to the whipping post. Making his way through the jeering crowd some minutes later, a soldier rushes up to Raffa and hands him a coiled long black whip. Raffa turns it over in his hand then hands it to Anton.

He whispers to Anton, "Are you sure about this?"

Anton looks at it and knows it is the very whip he had seen made not so long ago. Anton nods to Raffa as he handles the lengthy whip, he starts to unwind it, then walks back, as he counts off eight steps.

Not caring if anyone is noticing him, especially because of all the chaos going on around him, he knows most eyes are not on him but on Jesus. He drags the tail of the whip close to his hob-nailed boot. He then proceeds to step on the bone shards that are attached to it. He grinds his boot deep and imagines he hears the satisfying crunch of the bone and claws shattering that have been tied to the end of the whip.

Not only the shards are breaking up but as he grinds his heel into the ends of the whip and dirt, he can also feel some of the metal balls dislodging. He takes a deep breath, then slowly lets it out. In the back of his mind, he feels regret and a feeling of deep sorrow. He then rears back and strikes out with the whip to connect with Jesus' shoulder and back.

The inhumane crowd roars with excitement and begins to count, 5, 6, 7, it goes on and on, 16, 17, 18. As Anton wields the whip, the massive crowd screams, more, more, harder, harder.

Suddenly in the midst of all the madness, Anton cannot hear the crowd. It is as if the world has instantly become silent. A calmness befalls him. It was like nothing he had ever felt before.

Then, what seemed like only a few seconds later, as if awakening from a dream, Anton at once begins to hear the contemptible crowd again, 36, 37, 38. The screaming and yelling was louder than ever.

Exhausted, Anton stops and looks down at the blood that has splattered all over his arms and tunic from the backlash of the whip. Next, he looks and sees the blood-drenched, unrecognizable figure lying in a crumpled heap not more than ten feet in front of him. The brutal multitude of people are still cheering as if they expect more entertainment.

Anton sees Marcus, nods for him to come over. "Help me untie him, brother, I want to make sure he is still alive."

They both rush to Jesus. As Marcus is cutting the restraints from Jesus' wrist, Anton bends down to check to see if Jesus is breathing. With startling clarity, Jesus gazes into Anton's eyes and says, "Once you offered me water, today you showed me compassion. Now I offer you life."

Then Jesus sighed heavily in pain. Amazingly to Anton's surprise, Jesus' breath smelled like a combination of honey and the fragrant scent of fresh-cut flowers. The instant after taking in the scent of Jesus' breath, Anton was stunned for a second and could barely move.

In the next moment, as he shook off the dazed feeling, a group of soldiers appeared and there in their midst stood Pontius Pilate. He pointed to Jesus and ordered Marcus and Anton to stand him up. Coming around from the back of them, were four other soldiers from another company that the two brothers did not know.

They held something in their hands. Before anyone could say anything, one of the soldiers pushes a crown of thorns on Jesus' head, as another wraps a beautiful purple robe around his shoulders and hands him a long reed stick.

Marcus steps forward and starts to grab a hold of one of his fellow soldiers. "What do you think you are you doing? Has this man not suffered enough?"

"Pilate looks over at Marcus and grunts, "Move back and be silent, soldier!"

An instant later, Pilate turns around. Spreads his arms out and says to Joseph Caiaphas the high priest, along with the rest of the Pharisees and citizens standing around, "I have punished your king. Now let this be."

Caiaphas, looking like a madman shrieks, "This is no king of ours! The people of Jerusalem demand that you crucify this man. The Jewish High Council demands that he be put to death, that he be crucified."

At that point, the mob of people start screaming, crucify him! Crucify him! Crucify him! Pilate is now at his wit's end. Not paying attention to his wife's warnings, he concedes to the pressure of the Pharisees, if only to put the matter behind him.

"I will do as you wish but I do not condone this one bit. The emperor will surely hear of this."

Anton literally jumps forward and starts to protest to Pilate. "Sir, this is so wrong. How can you possibly condemn this man? There is absolutely no reason why this man should die."

Pilate, looking very tired replies, "Stand down soldier, you know nothing of this affair."

Then ignoring Anton as he starts to say something else, Pilate turns to the other soldiers that are standing there and commands them to do as they had been ordered. "And take that robe off him. He will not need it."

THREE NAILS AND A SPEAR

Anton feels devastated and he knows not why. On the way out of the courtyard following the rest of the soldiers, Marcus catches up to Anton. "Come on man, let's just do this."

Anton looks down and then grumbles, "No brother, I will not be going anywhere. I have not been ordered to do so; I will not make myself go. I would take no pleasure in seeing what they have in store for him.

We both have been awake for many hours and after the scourging, I have absolutely no energy left. You go and be a witness for both of us. I will go back to Antonia Fortress and ponder upon this day, a day that I know, neither of us will ever forget."

It is early afternoon, by the time Anton gets back to the fortress. For no other reason than he is dead tired, he can't keep his eyes open as he lays on his bunk and thinks about the day's events. As he slowly drifts off to sleep, he wonders what Jesus meant when he said to him, "I give you life."

Anton lays on his bunk asleep, he dreams of a white dove flying down from the sky towards him. As it draws near to him, Anton is suddenly awakened. He feels the whole building start to shake, rattle and roll, then a sound like thunder startled him even more. He quickly gets up to take a look outside and fines it to be dark as night even though it is only mid-day.

Most of the other soldiers were either somewhere resting or outside the fortress. He had no idea what was going on, as he turns the whole incident of the day over in his mind. He not only feels disoriented but very uneasy. Thinking he should feel shame and remorse about the circumstances of the day but strangely enough, he only feels a sense of contentment. As if something dark and dirty had been lifted from his heart and soul. What he feels is bliss.

After contemplating the events of the day a bit more, he gets off his bunk again and takes another look outside. It was starting to clear up, to become day again, he returns to his room. He just wants to lay on his bed and think.

It must have been several hours later when Marcus entered his room. He sees Anton sitting on the edge of his cot, so he goes over and sits on his own bed. Anton stares at him, seeing that he is practically in tears asks him, what is troubling you brother?"

"What a soldier I turned out to be."

Anton just watches him.

"Brother, I wept. I know we have seen others crucified before. Like that time just outside of Rome. When father took us to the market and they had left those four robbers strung up on crosses, down the road from the main gate. That was truly a horrible sight.

This time though, it was somehow different. I watched as they stripped off his clothes, leaving him naked then threw him to the ground and kicked him into position until He lay flat on the cross.

Two soldiers held his arms while another drove a nail into one hand then the other, a third nail was driven into his feet. For a moment I could not think, I mean it should not have been as emotional for me as it was. I am not exactly prone to violence. But each time that hammer fell, my heart would break a little more.

Anton, they tacked a sign above his head, It said, ''Jesus King of the Jews."

I watched that whole ordeal closely. I saw that Jew persecutor. The Pharisee, the one they call Saul of Tarsus."

Anton suddenly looks up at Marcus. "Of course, he was there. Why wouldn't he be? He has been persecuting those that follow the Way since we first arrived here. Today must have been his biggest triumph."

Marcus continues, Yes, you're absolutely right. He was right up there with a few Sadducees and others, yelling taunts at Jesus. Mocking and laughing at Him like everyone else.

Then a curious thing happened. I could see Jesus turn and look down at Saul's group, He then said something to them. I was too far away to hear what he had said, but Saul instantly dropped his head, turned and backed out of the crowd. It was a very strange response on his part.

Then Saul did something that was even stranger. He doubled back to the front of the crowd and in his hand, he held a long reed with a dripping wet sponge stuck to the end of it. He then lifted it up, but Jesus turned his head aside and would not let it touch his mouth."

"Everything was in slow motion. Like I was there, yet not there. Hard to explain. Then for some reason that I could not figure out, Longinus the centurion who oversaw our detail, after having words from another soldier, rode up on his horse and pierced Jesus through his side with a spear.

I later asked another soldier, why our centurion would have done that to Jesus only. He had no answer. I did realize that the spear he used was the one with the bronze tip. It was the very same one we both saw that night in the armory. The one Gallo had made, the one he was so proud of.

Then the most unusual thing of all happened. The second Jesus was pierced, blood and what looked like water burst from the side of his chest to spray a mist throughout the crowd below him. The air was filled with it. Longinus got covered with blood as it rained down upon him.

Rubbing his eyes, he frantically wheeled his stead around like he was trying to get his bearings so he could back out and run off, scattering people everywhere. But then in mid-stride, he suddenly pulled hard back on the horse's reins, sprung down from his horse, hit the ground and brother, when I say hit the ground, I mean literally. First, he kneels then goes flat out. I thought he was hurt or something. In the next moment, he raises up to his knees looks up at Jesus, lifts his arms high above his head the loudly proclaims "Lord what have we done! For surely, this is the Son of God!

That was when I lost it. I tell you, brother. Right then, I could not breathe. I felt like I was having some kind of a heart seizure. For an instant, I felt unbearable pain in my lungs and heart. And then, in a blink of an eye, the agony was gone. I broke down and wept like a child and no one even noticed.

Then things got really crazy. It felt like the earth was erupting upon itself. People started falling to the ground. There was thunder and lighting. As if that wasn't enough? The sun literally disappeared. One second it was there, the next second it was gone. It stayed like that for I don't know how long, maybe a couple of hours. Then just like it never happened, Marcus snaps his fingers, the sun returned just like that. And no Anton, it was not an eclipse."

"I believe you brother. If you can believe me, I know exactly what you were feeling."

Marcus then tells Anton, there were two others on crosses, left hanging to be thrown into the pit. Our captain and four other soldiers from another unit got direct orders to take Jesus down off the cross.

"I helped raise the cross up out of the hole. Then we slowly lowered Jesus to the ground. One soldier helped another as he took a pair of iron tongs and pried the nails out of Jesus' hands and feet. Then two Jews came and carried him away.

I guess they buried him right away, somewhere close by. I didn't follow them to see where. I ran into Raffa on the way back here. He looked in worse shape than I felt. He did say to get some well-earned rest."

GONE MISSING

Even though the boys were granted a two-day pass, they mostly stayed in the barracks. It was Sunday morning, the first day of the week. Anton, Marcus and Raffa were back on duty awaiting orders when the captain burst into their room and ordered them to follow him, then proceeded to enter each separate room and commanded the whole company to assemble outside at once.

After everyone had gathered in front of the fortress, the captain told his men, "I don't know when this insanity is going to end. Apparently, someone has removed Jesus' body from his grave. Perhaps it was stolen or maybe someone just reburied it someplace else. Whatever the case may be, I don't care! What I do care about is, I have been ordered by that pompous pig of a priest Caiaphas, to find Jesus' body and then present it to him. If Pilate himself had not sought me out personally and commanded that I obey Caiaphas' order, I would have gone and told, mister high-and-mighty priest to go and find the body himself.

Including some of the 3rd regiment, standing here before me, I see close to one hundred and twenty men. We cannot fail. We will not fail to find this man's body.

Your sergeant's orders are to divide his company into ten-man units. Traverse and search under every rock if need be. Every home, every inn, every stable. Tear this whole city apart if you must. Oh, and you can also bet the soldiers that were assigned to guard the tomb so as to prevent such a thing like this from ever happening and I'm not talking about the temple guards but those soldiers on my watch responsible for this travesty will not be seen around here again. Or for that matter around anywhere ever again. We are legionnaires, not irresponsible auxilia mercenaries."

Anton nudges Marcus, "I know they say he is not in the grave, but I found out where he was supposedly buried. It's by a garden not far from where they crucified him. Let's walk over there and look at the tomb anyway. Maybe we could get an idea, figure out what happened."

Not knowing where Raffa was, Anton and Marcus started out to where the soldier had told Anton, Jesus had been taken. It was not far from the mount called Golgotha, known to the soldiers as Calvary.

After walking a bit, they came to the garden and then spied out the entrance of the tomb maybe fifty feet away. Just before reaching it, they see a young woman, it looks to them like she just exited the entrance of the tomb. Wild-eyed, looking all around, she practically sprints right towards them.

Marcus puts his hands out and shouts, "Woman stop! Stop now!"

She pulls up right in front of them, barely able to breathe. She is crying, shaking and laughing at the same time.

Anton puts his hand on the woman's shoulder and says, "You are safe now. Take a deep breath, just relax for a minute. You're going to be okay. Who has assaulted you? Where is he? Are you hurt?"

Barely able to contain herself, but realizing the two soldiers have completely misunderstood, she blurts out, "He was just over there and points to a large rock. I'm not hurt at all.

At first, I did not recognize him. I thought he was the gardener and I asked him, please kind sir, where have you taken Jesus? He looked right at me. It seemed to me as if his whole image wavered and became pure light."

He said, "It is I, Jesus."

He looked into my eyes and said, "Mary, go and tell the others you have seen me."

"These tears you see now, they are tears of joy for he has risen.

Do you not understand? He has risen! Just as he said he would. Please let me pass. I must tell the others of the good news, the wonderful news! They must all learn of this immediately."

With that being said, she scooted past them and ran down the road in a flash. Marcus and Anton just stood in the middle of the garden path in awe.

"Brother, what now? Who in their right mind would ever believe us if we told anyone what we just heard, and from a woman no less?

Anton looks up at the clear blue sky. Not a cloud to be seen, and softly said, almost to himself. "I believe her."

"You are right Anton; I also can think of no reason why she would lie."

Back in their room, Anton was talking to Marcus and Raffa. "You realize growing up, all we ever heard, then in school, all we learned about the gods, Zeus, Venus, Apollo and all the rest of the stories, was rubbish. Was any of that even real? I think not.

Now, my heart tells me that they were all just myths, legends and way out fables, perhaps to frighten us or keep us all in line. They had no real substance and no proof of ever being real. All three of us have witnessed the works of Jesus.

Is it possible that we can go on denying him, even though we saw him perform miracles right before our eyes, we listened to the words he spoke. He even acknowledged that the words were not only his but the words of the one so vast, of one that dwells in all of us. All he asked of us was to repent of our sins, just change our sinful ways, believe and trust in him and now we have it firsthand that he has indeed risen from his grave."

"All I know is before I encountered him, before I looked into his eyes and before he spoke to me, in truth I was someone else.

We have witnessed and felt the power of his phenomenal abilities and seen his devotion to the people, not just the Jews but all people. At no time did he not radiate love, peace, and compassion for those around him. He would not even let his own disciples defend him."

"Do you not remember when we took him from the garden that night? He looked right at us, then looked at the disciple who had raised a sword and said to all that stood before him, if I asked? 'Do you not think my father would not provide me with more than twelve legions of angels?'

"I am quite sure he was serious. Now he is Resurrected. Already there have been rumors that people have seen him."

"Marcus and I did see that young lady running out of his tomb. Why is it so hard for anyone to believe that Jesus Christ is the Son of God? To me, it would seem much harder to believe that he was not. I for one feel it in every part of my being that I need to find his disciples."

Marcus and Raffa hadn't said anything, just sat there and listened to every word Anton was saying.

"I want to talk with them. To learn from them so I can share with others how he made me feel and what I witnessed."

Marcus finally speaks up, "Brother what are you saying? You know that if you tried to leave the army, they would hunt you down and kill you."

"Yeah, like they killed Jesus. I don't care. I will find his disciples and hope that they will deem me worthy enough to accept me. And you know what? Both of you are welcome to join me."

SEARCH PARTY

In the days that followed, Anton and his fellow soldiers patrolled not only their assigned areas but many of the other parts of the city as well. No matter where they looked or how hard they searched, no disciples of Jesus could be found. It was as if the ones that had believed in him and followed him had scattered throughout the land. It seemed they had all left Jerusalem.

It was about the 4th week after Jesus' crucifixion, while Anton and the others were patrolling the area, that Marcus had stopped and started to talk with one of the street-market vendors, when a boy barely out of his teens approached Marcus and said, "Can I speak to you alone for a moment?"

Marcus lead him off to the side of the stall and asked, "What is it?"

The boy replied, "I am told you seek information as to the whereabouts of the ones that follow the Way."

Marcus just stared at him. Anton and Raffa spotted Marcus and the boy conversing and started to walk over. The boy talking to Marcus glanced over but continued speaking.

"I have just returned from Galilee. You may find him there."

As the young man started to walk away, Marcus called to him, “Hey, you said, to find him? Not them. Who are you? You didn’t even ask for compensation for letting us know where they are.”

The youngster turned and walked back a few paces. My name is Mark. “You see, the Pharisees laugh and say all of Jesus’ disciples fled in terror after he was crucified. My friends, as with so many of the things the Pharisees speak of, that is not the truth. Yes, some of Jesus’ followers were scared and left Jerusalem in sadness and sorrow. Our hearts were broken. Some thought the chosen one had abandoned his people, others thought he was dead. That is simply not true. I stayed close by, witnessing all. My friend whom I call brother John not only witnessed our beloved in passing but was responsible to see that the Anointed One’s mother, Mary, was comforted. He did not leave her side.

And now those that follow him, know the truth, for He has risen. So, you see my compensation is in knowing there would be no way you and your friends would be seeking disciples of Jesus unless God’s Spirit was speaking to you. Your quest has only just begun. You will find the apostles of Jesus Christ. It was written long before you were born, those that believe and seek after the Lord will not perish but will have everlasting life.

With a knowing smile, the lad walked away and melted back into the crowded marketplace.

THE JOURNEY

Anton handed Marcus a pear, and said, "Brother I see you seek the Lord without even knowing it."

"Or perhaps, it is He that seeks me. And yes, little brother, I can almost feel what you're thinking. So, go ahead and say it."

Sure enough, just as he thought, it wasn't even two minutes after the boy had departed, that Anton clarified, "We do have a four-day pass coming up in a few days and wherein all the land should we go? If not to Galilee"

Galilee was some miles away from Jerusalem. The prestige that Anton hated but somehow acquired because of his role at the Antonia Fortress courtyard that fateful day, he easily procured two horses from a captain of a mounted unit. They rode till they came to the territory of Samaria, where they spent one night. The very next day they continued to Galilee.

Having reached Galilee in the mid-afternoon they checked into an inn that offered food and lodging. After a rather satisfying meal of grilled lamb, fresh cheese, fruit and a glass of the local wine, they refreshed themselves then rested for a brief time. Knowing that their uniforms could be intimidating, they changed into the common clothes they had brought with them so they might blend in with everyone else.

Earlier, having left their horses to be attended, Anton and Marcus now stepped out of their room, to see many people walking past the inn. It looked like they were heading to the outskirts of town.

Anton spoke softly, almost to himself, and said, "I wish Raffa was here with us. I kind of miss him."

The next moment, Marcus calls out from the doorway of their room to someone walking by. "Hey, where is everybody going?"

A comely middle-aged woman walking beside her large dog, replied to him, "We are going to the beautiful green slope at the Mount of Roses. "The Anointed One will speak there. You should come and listen. You would be very glad you did." After she answers, she turns and walks on.

The two brothers just look at each other. Anton comments, "Some things are just meant to be."

With a gallant sweep of his hand, Marcus says, "Shall we proceed?"

As they moved along with the others, in time they reached the bottom of the green. They were surprised to see so many people from all walks of life gathered in one very spacious area.

The grounds were covered with a soft layer of vibrant green grass leading to a gentle incline that could only be described as a gently flowing sea of roses. There were not only locals moving about but also many people from the outer regions as well. All were milling around, speaking with each other in a quiet manner as if waiting in anticipation for something special. There must have been at least three or four hundred people maybe more, some standing, others sitting or lying on the grass, talking to each other. All waiting.

DELIVERANCE

Marcus points out and says to Anton, "Hey, look over there, that fella looks familiar."

Anton agrees. "Isn't that the man that stood with us at the fire-pit when we were in the courtyard at Caiaphas' temple? Let's go over and have a little chat with him."

As they approach him, the man looked a bit uneasy.

"Sir, we thought we might have recognized you. We just wanted to say hello. What is your name?"

"I am Cephas. I was born Simon Peter. Yes, I do remember you now, even without your uniforms. You are legionnaires. You were both in the garden also, Anton not wanting to alarm anyone or cause any trouble, moves with Peter, away from the familiar-looking woman he was standing with, and says, "If I remember correctly, you told a few people, you did not know Jesus."

Marcus walks a little closer to them both, as Peter sighed, "What you say is quite true. I am not going to make any excuses. But perhaps I can at least explain. That night, I cannot tell you of the stress and anxiety I felt. Or how distraught I was. Please understand me when I tell you, I love this man with all my heart, with all my soul, and with all my strength.

This man is my friend, my teacher, and my Lord. You soldiers took him away that night. When the servant girl asked if I was with him? I automatically said no. I was desperately trying to figure out some way to rescue him. Does that sound absurd? Do you not remember that I stood before you in the garden and struck the servant's ear with my sword? Did you not see the blood that gushed out? And then in an instance... it was like it never happened!

My Lord reprimanded me that night. He told me to put away my sword. It was not needed. I did not understand how he could have said that to me. I would have gladly given up my life for him in a second. I was in a blur. I felt so helpless. I still had my sword when I was in the courtyard, but I was alone.

Then as they were bringing Him back out of that spurious trial, I heard the Pharisees' saying, now he will die, for he shall be crucified.

A great fear came upon me. Then others, maybe it was even you that started asking me if I was a disciple. I don't know, I was so wrong. I denied him again and again. I was a sad excuse for a man, I know that now.

I tried to talk myself into believing that if I was arrested or perhaps even killed, who would continue to tell those that did not know of the Messiah, that he indeed had come so that the world through him might be saved.

Like some others, I'll admit to you, as I admit to myself, that when Jesus was crucified, I was of little faith. I felt crushed. I truly thought they had killed him and that was it.

That was before. Now, not only has He resurrected but he has stood before me as I stand before you. And yes, I was truly ashamed that I had ever doubted."

When he looked into my eyes and said, 'Doubt is part of being human. In time you will learn to overcome it. For you no longer walk in the flesh but you now walk in the Spirit of God.' I felt my guilt and condemnation leave me. I only have room in my heart and in my soul for my Lord and Savior Jesus Christ."

From the back of where the three men stood talking, an unobtrusive voice gently spoke out.

"Cephas was forgiven even before he forgave himself."

Anton turned to look back. Because of the brilliance of the sunlight, he could not make out the indistinct image of the speaker's face. As the man stepped closer and they recognized him, both Anton and Marcus fell to their knees.

Jesus looked down and touched the shoulders of each man and said, "Please, both of you stand up. We need not have any of that here. You have knelt before me in your heart and in your soul, that is all I ask."

As they stood before Jesus, he steps in a bit closer to them.

Anton speaks softly to Him, "My Lord you have looked into my brother's heart as you have looked into mine. Your spirit has touched us both. I only ask now, and I speak for my brother also that you accept us into your company and let us follow you. Let us learn from you."

"You, my two friends have already been following me and you have been learning from me, every step of the way. What I am about to tell you is true. You may think that you want to disregard your calling as soldiers, regardless of the consequences.

Friends, your destiny does not include leaving the army but embracing it. You both are mighty warriors. You are both soldiers, pure of heart, that I know. Many in your ranks are lost but cry out to be found. Both you and your companions are greatly needed right where you are.

You are witnesses to my work and of my words. Share with others what you have seen and what you have heard. For as to the events you have witnessed, they have changed your lives. You, in turn, will greatly influence other lives. Share with your fellow warriors, lead those whose destiny will be to believe in me, as you believe in me.

You will have much work to do and as I ascend to be with the Father, a short time from now, I will leave you both a helper. The Holy Spirit will dwell inside you and guide your way to salvation. Verily I say unto you, soon both of you will return to Rome. Once there, you will seek out a centurion by the name of Julius Cassius. He knows you by his dreams and he awaits your arrival. Both you and your friends, along with his band of believers, will do much good work in this world.

Your travels will exceed your expectations. For you will carry the word of God and your love for me to the far corners of this earth.

After embracing each of the two young men, Jesus turns and as the crowd begins to part for him, he goes about and through the mass of humanity gathered there. As he climbs halfway up the gentle slope, enveloped by the scent of roses, he turns towards the people and faces the multitude of eyes looking at him.

There came upon all that were together that day a great silence. Jesus spread both of his arms out above his head and said, in a voice that all could hear.

"In the name of my Father and of the Holy Spirit, today beloved, for those that believe, for those that will believe, be blessed with the grace of God.

For what I'm about to say is true... And He began to speak."

The beginning

THE GOLDEN BOX

PROLOGUE

Just outside the city in a small field, many people had converged. Pushing and shoving one another, the large crowd consisted mostly of the citizens of Jerusalem. Everyone seemed to be jostling for a position this day. Standing silently on the sidelines, Pharisees, Scribes, and an array of Roman soldiers were all watching the gathering. Four of the Pharisees, as if obeying a signal of some sort, stepped forward and began to intermingle with the crowd.

The people that had assembled for this event were a clamorous bunch. They could be heard from afar yelling, screaming taunts and obscenities at the three men suspended high above them. Those that had arrived early, stood closest to the foot of the cross, practically underneath the man in the center. They stared up at him in horror. Tears flowing, weeping openly, as if in dire pain themselves.

The man looked down at them. He gasped for breath. His face, a portrait of pain and misery, bloody and unrecognizable except for his eyes. He slowly lowered his head down and looked at those below him. He then raised his head up and gazed out across the field, at the multitude of people watching him. Grimacing in pain and suffering, he then arched his back and labored to take in one last breath of air.

In a surprisingly strong and clear voice, he proclaimed the words, "Father it is finished."

As his eyes close, an unnatural calm fall upon the crush of people.

There are no birds chirping, no braying of donkeys nor barking of dogs. Not a voice to be heard...utter soundlessness. A blanket of the deepest silence covered the entire area. It seemed as if the world was standing still.

Then, in a blink of an eye, it began... just the tiniest of vibrations. Like the physical sense, one feels when a cold chill runs through their body, followed by a gently swaying sensation that could be felt underfoot.

Even though the mass of people milling around were trying to keep their balance, some grabbed hold of each other, while others stumbled around as if they were drunk.

Gathering momentum like a ponderous wave that slowly rolls with massive power and then slams into the bow of a ship, the earth rumbles, groans, and begins to heave. Like a newly active volcano, it literally erupts upon itself. Spontaneous pandemonium breaks out. Screaming and crying in terror can be heard throughout the city. Those in the field try to run back toward the city's gate, only to be tossed about and thrown violently to the ground like rag dolls.

Those few who knew him, sink to their knees. They felt no dread, only anguish and grief. They knelt below his cross and touched it's beam, for it had stood steady and sound throughout nature's onslaught. Holding each other's hands, they bow their heads together and vehemently prayed, as the daylight began to fade, and the world plunged into total darkness.

THE BEGINNING

30 AD

Dazzlingly intense flashes of lightning, followed by rolling thunder, was as deafening as the sound of a gigantic avalanche of granite boulders and huge blocks of ice being crushed together while cascading down a mountainside.

It was ear-splitting, booming every few seconds, accompanied by even more flashes of lightning. The earth shuddered vigorously, like a pride of a thousand lions shaking themselves dry after a storm. The sun completely disappeared from sight and the world was left in darkness.

On top of a desolate hillside just outside of Jerusalem, four women and two men now huddled on their knees in the mud and rain.

They had taken their cloaks, shaw's and coats off, so as to cover each other the best they could. Between heart crushed weeping, they prayed passionately as they held each other's hands. It might have been just over an hour or so that all the surrounding lands had stayed in total darkness.

Although to those on that hilltop, it felt much longer. Then in an instant, as if a colossal black curtain had suddenly been withdrawn, the sun reappeared.

The two men helped the women as they slowly rose up and uncovered themselves, for the rain had slowed to a drizzle and then to a light mist. In unison, they turned their heads up and beheld the one they all had become to know as their Messiah.

He was a son to one of the women. Companion, teacher and much more to the others that had gathered with her. Just as they started moving about, another woman rushed across the strangely deserted area of the mostly abandoned field.

The one called Joanna, slowed down when she spotted them. Then she continued walking closer to them and nodded to the four other women as she approached them. One of the women standing there, named Salome embraced her. The other three all happened to be named Mary, they stood there, and each gave her a hug one at a time.

"Sisters, I'm so glad I've found you. Everything got so dark. It was like I was blind; I could not see anything in front of me. I was very disoriented until the sun returned. Blessed sisters, you all know me, we all feel deeply pained. The agony is tearing at our hearts and souls but did He not tell us"–-At that very moment a half a dozen Roman soldiers, a Centurion, along with two other men, approached the group of women standing alone by the cross that held Jesus.

After receiving an order brought by a carrier directly from Pontius Pilate and having made sure that Jesus was indeed dead, the well-known Centurion Longinus ordered four of his soldiers to raise the main column of the cross up and out of the earth's cavity.

The Centurion rubbed both of his eyes and in a strangely soft-spoken voice said, "Move back. Move away from here. This is no place to stand."

Pointing up at Jesus, he snapped, "Let my soldiers bring that man down."

The rest of the soldiers helped to steady the cross. Then working together, they slowly brought Jesus down with the cross. Laying it flat on the ground in order to be able to wrench out the nails that had been hammered through his hands and feet, as the nails were deeply embedded into the thick wood of the cross.

The five women all started to move towards the side of the field, one of the Mary's, the one called Mary Magdalene, glanced back at the two citizens that had accompanied the soldiers.

She did a double-take, shook her head, then in an accusing voice says, "I know you. I know both of you, don't I?"

You are a Pharisee, and you are an official that hides in the shadow of the Jewish council. What do you want with him now?"

Both men hung their heads in shame, as the other women look accusingly at them.

Another woman speaks up. "Mary, what you say is true. She looked directly at one of the men. "I remember you were with him one evening as he spoke to a small group."

"I am Joseph of Arimathea and yes we knew him. I was ignorant. I was dead wrong not to confess my love, my devotion to him. Both my dear friend Nicodemus and I know it was a grave mistake of the worst kind not to speak out in his defense. I was a coward. The other council members would have condemned us both. We were fearful and now we are humiliated and guilty of denying him.

We have come to give him a proper burial such as he so deserves. Truthfully, we had no idea what Caiaphas was up to. We knew he wanted Jesus punished for blasphemy, for sharing a new doctrine. But to order his death? And who would have ever thought that Pilate would have condoned such madness? By the time we found out what was happening, there was absolutely nothing we could have done to stop it." Joseph finishes speaking to Mary Magdalene.

Salome gets their attention. Points a finger at the soldiers, as they are lying Jesus still nailed to the cross onto the ground. Joseph and Nicodemus turn and hasten towards the cross. The women also start to drift over as well.

They can now see one soldier kneeling beside Jesus' body. The women gradually move closer. They see that the soldier has a pair of iron tongs in his hands and is fastening them to the head of the nail that has pierced Jesus' hand. He grasps the top of the oversized nail as another soldier kneels beside him and overlays the end of the cross beam with a thick flattened metal bar. He then expertly slides the bar between Jesus' outstretched hand and the nail. He presses downward as the other man twists and pulls the tongs up. With a bit of effort, the nail is slowly drawn out. As the nail slides out, the soldier picks it up, looks at it, shakes his head and tosses it out into the wet muddy ground.

The two soldiers change positions and start in on the next nail. Not paying attention to the women that have been staring at them. Having completed their task, they get up and walk over to the other condemned men.

Joseph immediately steps forward. "Ladies, we must prepare our Lord. Those soldiers standing over there by that large rock, they want to escort us to where we shall bury Jesus. I know not why.

I have arranged a resting place for him, just beyond the garden. Let us go now before they change their minds and have us bury him somewhere else."

Joseph is still speaking to Nicodemus as they start to wrap Jesus in linen. Nicodemus, "You are going to have to help me carry him. I do not want any of these soldiers touching him."

Nicodemus responds, "As if they would even bother helping us.

My friend, you do know what they just did with the other two that were beside him? Joseph, just a few seconds ago I saw four soldiers hauling them off to a pit that they had prepared earlier. Our esteemed colleagues wanted no one left hanging out here, because of the Sabbath. These soldiers, are unbelieving pagans with hearts of stone."

Joseph ignores the comment, then responds with, "We will cover him with the linen we have brought and arrange him correctly when we get to the tomb, I have set aside for him." The two men start to lift the body.

Mary the mother of Jesus says to Joseph, "My friend John escorted two elders to the gate. "He will return for me in just a few minutes. If you might wait? He can also help."

Joseph shakes his head and replies, "Mary we have got to go now. Those soldiers are not going to let us wait. They do not want to be here with us one second longer then they have to be. We need to be on our way immediately. Can you women give us a hand? Please help carry these satchels of spice and scented oils. Be very careful for the oils are a bit heavy."

Mary Magdalene answers, "Of course we will. It is getting so cold out here. We do need to be on our way."

They all start the short walk towards the garden. As the five women begin to follow the men down the path to the garden, Joanna steps to the side of the path and tells the others to go on ahead.

She quietly whispers to Mary the wife of Clopas, "Let the other women know that I will catch up to them. There is something I must do. There is something I have forgotten."

Thinking nothing more of it, the women continue on their way. Joanna gives it a few seconds then turns around and hurries back toward the small hill where Jesus had been crucified. She walks on the muddy ground passing the disregarded lengths of rope used to tie the two other convicts to their crosses. The beams themselves lay broken and tossed to the side. Lying on the wet churned up ground, like so many pieces of timber.

Joanna approaches the third cross, which is lying in the dirt separated from the others. She now starts to look all around the area. Everything is still very wet. The ground is like a quagmire. It looks as if a large herd of animals had trampled all through it. She starts to concentrate and begins her search but sees nothing of interest.

Nearing the cross, she now goes down on all fours. On her hands and knees, she starts to wave her hands across the ground scooping up small handfuls of dirt. Another and another and another. Dirt and mud are flying in every direction. Desperate to seek what she is searching for she does not hesitate and just keeps clawing at the ground.

"Yes!" Finally, she feels an object and quickly tucks it into her smock.

She moves over to the other side of the cross, drops to her knees once again and starts to perform the same movements as before. Not finding what she is seeking, methodically she sifts through the squishy soil and is finally rewarded.

A short distance away a man walks towards her. She is startled and slowly raises to her feet as he says, "So, what do we have here? There is nothing here of any value my child, but did I see you pick something up?"

"As you say, sir. Nothing of value here but what is that you have in your hand?"

With a wave of the small wooden plaque in his hand, he does not answer but just saunters off. Joanna looks all around her before falling to the ground and once again starts kneading her fingers through the mud.

She now moves on down by the foot of the cross and meticulously starts the painstaking procedure one more time. The sun is beginning to set. It will soon be dark once again.

For the young woman, the minutes have turned into more than an hour. It is not the frustration of not finding what she is looking for, but because she is beginning to become very weary; it has been a horrific day. Vowing not to quit looking, she continues searching in an ever-widening circumference.

Becoming a bit distressed, doubt starts to trickle into her mind. Joanna stops for a minute. She looks up just as the sun is beginning to go down. It looks stunning, serene, so majestic. She raises her hands up above her head, begins to praise God and give thanks.

She closes her eyes and as the tears begin to flow. It seems from somewhere far away, she hears a small quiet voice, "Fear not my child, you will be safe in this life here on earth, and in your next life also. I am with you always."

Her eyes immediately flash open. She turns her head this way and that but sees no one. She quickly brings her hands down to the ground to raise herself up. Her left-hand lands on the very thing she had been hunting for. She wraps her fingers around it and slowly, reverently lifts it up to the fading light of dusk. In Joanna's mind, it felt like she had uncovered one of the world's greatest gifts. For she had finally found the third nail used to crucify Christ Jesus.

RESTING

Joanna walks beside a small brook on her way to the garden. She sees the clear calm water and crouches down, with the intention of washing the nails off that are caked with mud and blood.

She takes one of the nails out of her pocket. She feels a small vibration and shutters as a subtle feeling of warmth surrounds her. Suddenly she pulls her hand back and for a reason unknown to her decides not to wash the nails off.

Joanna arrives at the tomb to see the four women along with Joseph and Nicodemus still gathered around Jesus.

Nicodemus softly says, "We have prepared the Anointed One with spices and a mixture of myrrh and aloes. It is not a pleasant scent?"

Joseph comments, "We will leave him in peace now. We shall let him rest."

Joseph passes Clopas' wife Mary, he hands her the bloodied linen.

She glances down and gasps, for she is not only shocked but stares in amazement at the blood-stained image of Jesus. Mary stands up holding the burial cloth, she stretches it out to its full length and shows it to her friend Mary Magdalene and then to Jesus' mother Mary and Salome. She then carefully folds the linen and puts it in her satchel.

Everyone is stirring about as if coming out of a dream state. The two men start for the entrance.

Mary the mother of Jesus looks over at the two men and quietly says, "Thank you both, for what you have done."

Joanna then states, "I wish to have a word with my friends here, perhaps we shall see you both again. Everyone truly appreciates what you have done this night... Shalom."

Once the two men departed, Joanna and the others slowly start to move toward the entrance of the tomb. Joanna slows down and then stops.

"My friends, please come closer. Gather around, I have something to show you." She takes the nails out of her pocket and opens her hand; she then looks at each one of the four women.

"We are united in our Lord; she shows the nails to each of them. I went back to the cross and searched until I found each one. Mary was his mother and you two knew him the longest. I want each one of you to have one nail. Perhaps as an heirloom, a symbol, a remembrance or a memoir.

To be passed down to your children or to your children's children. The four women present glanced at each other. The three that were named Mary began to shake their heads, while Salome stood silent and listened.

Mary, Jesus' mother spoke up, Joanna? "None of us that are here this night, nor any of our families will ever forget Jesus for who he was or what he stood for. You were inspired by God to go back and collect those nails. I for one, do not think they should be separated. They are not only physical evidence of his suffering, but they are a symbol of his sacrifice to the world. Many would want to destroy them if they knew that they existed and what they stood for.

I think I speak for my sisters also. You were the one given the authority by God to ascertain the three nails. To claim them for us all.

We would like you to be the guardian of those precious nails, to be passed down through your lineage. You keep them safe in remembrance of Jesus who walked this earth with us, died so that our sins may be forgiven, and we will have eternal life with Him in Heaven."

The women looked over at the man lying peacefully on the slab of marble stone. The abrasions, deep bruises and cuts seemed to have dissipated. It looked as if he were merely asleep.

They continued to walk through the entrance and started to depart from the tomb. Mary Magdalene stopped the women for a moment. They turned together and looked back to see a few temple guards and three soldiers roll a huge stone in front of the entrance of the tomb. Then the temple guards bound the large round stone with heavy rope. The soldiers then posted up on both sides of the tomb as if they were guarding something.

THE BIG MOVE

Present Day

Little Dee, as her mother still liked to call her, even though her 17th birthday was just around the corner, was a typical fun-loving east coast teenager. Dee and her mother had always been very close. With her mother's long curly blond hair, ice-blue eyes and athletic body they looked more like sisters than mother and daughter.

Dee had what some folks might call a carefree life. It seemed as if it had always been just her and her mom.

Her father, whom she vaguely remembered had been a free spirit of the '90s. He had passed on after an unfortunate motorcycle accident when she was only five years old.

It was through her grandmother's assistance and tight-knit loving relationship with both her and her mother, that helped them persevere through hard times.

Dee's mother, whose name was Joanna, had turned her creative writing abilities into an online success, creating and contributing articles and blogs for two major newspaper columns. Financially back on her feet, she decided that she and her daughter would move from their small apartment in Somerville, New Jersey to Northern California.

Joanna's mother who was a retired schoolteacher had moved out to California two years earlier. Joanna had missed her mother dearly. She knew it was time for both her and Dee to have her mother closer.

Through an associate realtor friend of hers, Joanna was given an opportunity to buy a cute two-bedroom house in Northern California, just a few miles from her mother. The location of the place was called Willow Glen in the city of San Jose, twenty minutes away from where her mother lived in a beautiful area, known as Saratoga.

Not only was she getting a great deal on the house but being that it was close to where her grandmother had finally settled, she was quite excited about the move.

Dee was absolutely thrilled to be coming to Cali. Growing up on the east coast had been a lot of fun. It seemed there was never a dull moment but the friends that she hung out with all through high school were getting ready to graduate and moving on to different colleges. She would surely miss Summerville, still, she was ready for a change.

When Joanna first inquired about Willow Glen, the realtor described it as an upscale, peaceful part of town. He told her it had a solid well-established community. Having all the amenities of a big town.

Everything was quite convenient and with a large modern mall just six miles down the road, the realtor thought she would be quite happy with the location.

It was right on the money. Through the videos and photos of the home, it looked beautiful. The house was surrounded by a good-sized grass filled yard. There were two princely shade trees standing guard at the entrance and a variety of flowers in colorful arrangements. Someone had taken the time and effort to care for the place.

NEW TERRITORY

The house was just as beautiful as they knew it would be. With Willow Glen High School being only fifteen minutes away, Dee quickly found out that she could either ride her bicycle or walk to school from home.

The school itself seemed casual. It was her last year. It appeared to her that a lot of the kids in her classes just wanted to be done with school, so they could do what they called, 'The Big Escape' and that was to leave town once they graduated.

Dee thought she would like it here and couldn't see what the big rush was all about. She could understand the need to experience new things and new places. She was just grateful that her mom had scored such a cute house and being so close to the school was an extra advantage. Dee was very content, and things were going quite well. She had even made a couple of friends at school.

Then one Friday afternoon just after school as she was walking home, talking on her phone to one of her girlfriends from back east, when she glanced back and noticed two boys walking behind her. She had spotted them earlier, sitting in the back of one of her classes. She thought nothing of it until she started to hear them making comments.

When they got a little closer one yelled," Hey cutie, what's your name?"

Dee turned her head back for a second, not missing a beat and snapped, "My name's Dee."

She didn't stop, she just kept on walking, telling her friend on the other end of the cell, that she'll call her later, right now she's got to deal with a couple of idiot-boys that are walking behind her.

One of the kid's snickers, "That's a nice-looking iPhone you got there. It looks new. What model is it?"

Dee ignores the boys, keeps walking.

"What did it run you? About $800? Who were you talking to?"

She retorts, "You don't want to know."

As she turns into her yard, the first kid shouts out, "We know who used to live here. He was a little wuss, and nobody liked him."

Just then, Joanna opens the door. "Who's that?" Pointing to the two boys that had kept on walking down the street.

"No one." Dee replies, "Just a couple of kids from school." Dee thought no more of it, as she gave her mom a big hug.

GRAM

The weekend had finally arrived. Dee was looking forward to visiting her grandmother. She knew that her mother was also very excited about the prospect of seeing her mother. Her grandmother lived about 20 minutes away in a small ranch-style house with two other elderly friends.

Her grandmother and her two housemates from back in New Jersey had pooled their money together and bought a very comfortable spot here in sunny California.

It was a short drive on the freeway, down to Old Highway 9, then on to the outskirts of Saratoga. It was beautiful, the redwood trees, the overgrowth of pine and cedar. It was a wonder to look at the forest of different shades of green and the other earthly colors.

When Dee and her mom found the beautiful house tucked between a plethora of trees and wildflowers, they knew that they were at the right place. Her grandmother rushed out the door to greet them. It was all hugs, kisses, laughter, and tears. They hadn't seen each other in quite a while.

Dee thought that her grandmother for being almost sixty years old was quite spry. More agile than some of her mom's friends that were much younger, and not to mention she was still quite beautiful.

Her grandmother, whose name was Martha had startling blue eyes, weighed about one-thirty and stood five feet nine. Martha had no trouble looking most anybody in the eye while she spoke to them. She was imposing in her own right not looking anywhere near her age. Grandmother was also a great conversationalist and always had very cool stories to tell.

The visit that day was epic and both Dee and her mother promised to make time and see Martha every chance they could. After all, one of the major reasons for coming to California in the first place... was to be close to Gram.

Sometimes Dee's mother was busy or had a deadline with something she was working on and couldn't get out of it so she would drop her daughter off for the day in Saratoga.

Dee felt that her grandmother was such a sweetheart and one of the kindest people she had ever met. They would always have lunch, then do a bit of shopping in the small town. Perhaps even take in a movie.

Dee recalled the first time they went out to eat. It was lightly sprinkling, somewhat cold and as they were riding in the Uber together, on their way to one of her grandmother's favorite restaurants, they passed a woman on the side of the road. Standing under an umbrella with her three small children, she was selling fruit in boxes. Her grandmother shouted to the Uber driver to stop and backup. There happened to be no one else on the road at the moment. She opened the car door, stepped out and asked the women, "How much?"

The lady replied, "The tangerines are only $3 a bag. The oranges are the same price and the plums, I can give them to you for $2 a bag."

My grandmother said, "No, no. How much for it all?"

The startled woman stammered, "All? All the fruit? I don't know, maybe $100."

I was astounded as I watched my grandmother pull out two $100 bills from her purse and hand them to the women saying, "Get these children home. This is no weather for them to be out in."

Before the lady could even respond, Gram was back in the car. The door closed. We were on our way.

More than one incident like that happened when I was with her. I was always excited to hang out with her. I would never know what kind of adventure she would conjure up for me when I least expected it.

I always looked forward to seeing her.

PRIORITIES

On Thursday after school, Dee was at home on her laptop, when her mom came into her room. "I just got a call from your grandmother. She remembered it is going to be your birthday next Wednesday. She knew that we probably had something planned but wanted to know if you'd like to spend Saturday and Sunday out at her place, mentioning she had just bought two new baby chickens and the cutest potbelly pig.

I think she wants you to go to church with her on Sunday. She asked me if we had found a church to attend yet. I told her we have checked out a few but hadn't decided on one. I could hear the tone of her voice. It sounded like she didn't quite believe me. She commented on how she had not missed church in years. Told me, it gave her peace of mind to know for certain our Lord is always near and added we both needed to get serious."

Dee looked at her and said, "Well mom, you know she is right. We both have been lagging on going to church, haven't we?"

Joanna shrugged her shoulders and murmured, "You're right. It's just that I've been so busy every day by the time Sunday rolls around, I just want to rest. I don't feel like doing much of anything.

"Mom, I don't think that excuse would go over quite so well with Gram."

A WAR STORY

"Honey, did your grandmother ever talk to you about your Uncle John?" Joanna asked her daughter.

Dee thinks for a moment. "He was in the Marines, right? And he died?" She shakes her head. "No, not really. I mean I know Gram mentioned him before. He was in the service, but she never really talked to me about him."

Joanna is lost in her own thoughts for a moment then said, "He was older than me. I'll tell you one thing she never stopped missing him. I'd always see her looking at all the old photos of him and her together. My brother was a very good-looking man. It's been quite some time since I've thought about him. He was a medic in Desert Storm, during the Gulf War.

I'm surprised she hasn't brought him up to you yet. She never gets tired of reminiscing about her only boy. John was what they called a conscientious objector. He refused to carry a weapon. That kind of attitude is still frowned on, even now. Once, his superiors confronted him and asked him how he could possibly think he could be on a battlefield without a weapon.

Gram told me that he stood right up to them and told all those officers he had joined the military out of respect for his country. He stood in front of them and said, "There was a heroic soldier that served in the army in World War ll, by the name of Desmond Doss."

Desmond once said, "I joined the army to save lives not to take lives. He went on to say, "I love my country and my fellow man, but I love Jesus Christ and I will do my best to serve him first."

"My brother died in Desert Storm." Gram told me she was never prouder of him when an officer of the United States Marine Corps presented her with his Purple Heart and the Medal of Honor for bravery beyond the call of duty. Also telling her how her son had told the brass of Desmond's Doss' story. She said, "all the medals in the world wouldn't have changed his belief in his Lord and Savior."

Dee wiped away a solitary tear, while her mom wasn't looking and said, "He sounded like someone I would have liked to have known."

QUALITY TIME CELEBRATION

Dee's 17th birthday came and went. Wednesday, after school her mom took her to a farmer's market where they stopped and looked at a variety of things the vendors had for sale at the booths, kiosks and tents. There were some interesting items to look at Including lots of fresh fruits and vegetables. They ended up buying a scoop of their favorite ice cream, a leather purse that Dee thought looked retro, and a large bouquet of pink roses and bright sunflowers.

Sitting on an old wooden park bench, Dee and her grandmother began reminiscing about their wonderful moments shared together, while listening to a country band performing in the Downtown Historic Square. After wandering around a bit more, they end up having dinner at a casual Greek style restaurant.

Her mother gave Dee three different gift cards, in a pop-out greeting card, featuring a smiling clam that said, "I SHELL always love you."

Dee and two of her girlfriends hit the mall the very next day after school. Happy to spend every dime that was on her cards.

Saturday morning was bright and sunny. Dee and her mom pulled into one of the small parking spaces just outside the house. Martha was already outside waiting for them.

After big hugs and kisses for both, Gram pulls back, "Shrieks out, happy 17th sweetie!"

Lowering her voice, she says, "I am just so glad you both came this early."

She looked at her daughter Joanna, "I do hope you can stay for a while. My house-mates are out for the weekend and I cooked something special for tonight."

Joanna sighs and in a soft voice says mom, "I'm way behind on some work. My deadline is on Monday and I've got a lot of research to do. I wanted you to share this day with your granddaughter. I'll be back Sunday evening to pick Dee up. Perhaps we can have dinner then."

With a hug, a kiss and a quick goodbye for both, Joanna was off.

"Come on, I want to show you something." Martha walked Dee around the side of the house towards the back. "I'm going to introduce you to a new friend of mine named Harold."

Sure enough, there he was. Just standing there looking at them. Harold was the potbelly pig her mother had mentioned. Miniature in size, he almost looked like a small hairless dog.

Martha says, "Go on and pet him. He likes it when you talk to him. I bring him in the house whenever I have time for him. He's so friendly, he is like one of the family now."

Dee starts to giggle. "I can't help it." She starts laughing harder. She's laughing so hard now, she's holding her stomach and her eyes were starting to tear up. "Gram stop it. I can't take it anymore." She finally gets herself under control. "I thought you were going to show me something else. Like if you were going to show me a horse or a cow."

All the time Harold was just looking at her, with a very serious face. But hey, he sure was cute.

"Oh, there's the baby chicken's mom was telling me to watch out for. I think she thought they'd bite. She probably hasn't ever been around chickens."

Martha just chuckles and says, "Oh, your mom has definitely been around chickens before. Come on, I'll give you the tour."

As they both start to walk out back, Martha points over to a small wooden structure, that's the barn, it's locked up. The key is around here somewhere but right now let me show you the little brook that runs behind it."

Dee commented, "Who bothers locking up a barn?"

Martha doesn't answer just smiles and walks on.

The birthday dinner was excellent. It consisted of thinly sliced sirloin steak marinated in crushed Asian apples in a bit of lime and honey. Added to that, was Martha's rendition of coconut shrimp in mango salsa. She called her unique combination, surf, and turf. The dessert was just as yummy. French vanilla raisin ice cream over a homemade combo of blueberry, raspberry, and mulberry pie. After relishing that mini banquet, Dee was ready to just kick it, hear a story or two and hit the sheets.

Even though Dee was kind of expecting it, the Sunday morning wakeup call came a little too early.

Her grandmother came into the spare room, looking like she'd been up for hours and asked if Dee would perhaps like to accompany her to church. Gram said, "This particular church has a very nice prayer worship band." It consists of two guitars, a drummer and a singer. The acoustics are superb and the girl that sings has a voice like an angel.

Dee said, "Of course I will go with you. I'd love to" Then she thought to herself yeah, I really do want to go.

The church was midsize, kind of quaint and sat just inside the middle of town, what the locals would call Saratoga proper. A good amount of people had attended but it was not overcrowded. Yes, the band not only sounded excellent, but the lyrics were also heartfelt.

It turned out to be a beautiful morning. Dee was very glad that she had gone to the service with their grandmother. She hoped they would do it again soon.

SALVATION

Sunday afternoon, Dee and her grandmother had lunch at a cozy little restaurant called the Plumed Horse. It was fine dining at its best and was located near the gateway to the Santa Cruz mountains. After a grand meal, they ended up taking a Checker Cab back to Martha's house. Both decided to sit on the porch for a while and just chat.

Dee got a call from her mom telling her that instead of coming tonight to pick her up she was going to have to pick her up early tomorrow morning.

Dee let her grandmother know what her mom had said, "Something came up that she had to take care of and she'll be here bright and early tomorrow morning, so you're stuck with me tonight."

Dee sits down beside her grandmother in a large rattan chair.

Martha turns to her and softly says, "Thank you for coming to church with me today."

She adds, "It seemed like you enjoyed it. You know, if you really trust God's will, you must put every bit of your hope and faith in him. I'm afraid it's not as easy as just going to church occasionally. It's going to take a lot more effort on your part then just attending church or reading the bible in your spare time. That is not just what God asks of us. What do you really know about Jesus?"

Dee answers, "I know He is the son of God. He died on the cross for us."

Martha takes a deep breath, "That is a good start. When I was young, I thought that very same thing. I thought that was all there was to it. Just be a good person. Don't do anything stupid, help others when I could.

Dee, that is all good. I truly thought that was my ticket to Heaven.

Until someone very special showed me the Way. That person was your grandfather. There is so much more than just knowing about Jesus Christ. At some point, through spiritual guidance, someone that wants to believe will learn to open their heart, their soul and ask that the worldly veil be removed, that their spiritual eyes and ears be opened. Jesus will always be with you. He will never forsake you. But because of our free will, we must voluntarily ask him into our hearts."

Dee sits next to her grandmother and listens to her. She doesn't say a word.

"Granddaughter let me ask you a simple question. If you died tomorrow and came to stand before God and he asked you, why should I let you into heaven? What would you say?"

Dee answers, "I'd say, I've been a good person. That I've never hurt anyone, I tried to help those that I could. I'd say, I even gave money to the church when I went. Gram, I guess I really don't know what I'd say."

"Child, the bible tells us that by grace we have been saved through faith. That means recognizing, understanding and giving your life to Jesus you will be saved.

Through knowledge and spiritual wisdom, you will learn why he gave his life for us. He gave his life up so you and I would be forgiven for all our sins, past, present and future.

Watch me, maybe this will help you to understand and remember, raise your right hand."

Dee slowly raises her hand up and says, "Like this?

"Yes, keep your hand up. Touch your thumb with your other hand's index finger. From now on, that thumb is going to represent God's grace, like if you were hitch-hiking for a free ride. Grace is a free gift; grace means unmerited favor. Grace is not deserved and cannot be earned.

Next is your forefinger, your index finger. This one represents mankind. All people are sinners and they cannot save or forgive themselves. We have all fallen short of the glory of God.

The middle finger represents God. Which is apropos, as some unbelievers like to show their disdain, as well as their ignorance by lifting up their middle finger when asked about God. He is the God of love, but he is also the God of justification. He hates sin. That is why he sent his Son to die on the cross for our sins.

The fourth finger, the ring finger represents Jesus. He was 100% man and he is 100% God. As believers, we are in a marriage to Christ Jesus. We are bonded to him.

The last finger, the little finger represents faith...Because we have so little of it. Some evangelists call this the gospel hand. I just think it's a simple way to convey a bit of understanding to someone interested in learning and remembering God's way.

I know when I start talking sometimes, I can't stop but I'd just like you to remember this and even share it with others when the occasion arises."

"Gram, thank you for sharing that with me. I won't ever forget it."

"Dalene, I know your mother always calls you Dee, but your name is special and has meaning. I'm going to share one more thing with you today. It's not how often you go to church, read your Bible or how good you are. All those things should be done out of gratitude, honor, praise, and glory for the one that gives eternal life to those who believe in him.

I know you love Jesus. I want you to learn how to love him with all your heart, your mind, and your strength. You must ask him into your life if you want to truly be saved. Do you think you might want to do that?

Dee whispers, "I'm just not sure. Do you think he would accept me?"

"Oh yes child, I'm sure he will. He has been waiting for you.

Can you feel his presence here? The Bible says where two or more are gathered, I will be in your midst."

"I do feel it." A warm comfortable glow seemed to fill the whole room.

Gram, I would very much like to ask Jesus into my heart today."

Martha, through mist-filled eyes, said, "Little D, you must be sure because I am not so certain it will be easy for you if you choose this road.

If we are to see each other after we leave this world? There is no other way. Dee just nods her head yes.

"Dalene, repeat this prayer after me.

"Father God I believe your only son died on the cross for my sins. I believe he was resurrected from the dead and he is the eternal Son of God. Right now, I offer my humble repentance. I asked Jesus to come into my heart. I ask for a new beginning, a new life. Bless me with the Holy Spirit. For I know by the grace of God, through Jesus' torment, suffering and crucifixion, I am forgiven. My salvation has been provided. I will be granted the keys to the kingdom of heaven. In Jesus' name, I pray. Amen."

Tears flowed from both their eyes. Martha reaches over and tightly hugs her granddaughter.

Dee sits on the couch, as her grandmother stands up and quietly says, "Stay here for a minute I'll be right back I have something I've been waiting for a very long time to give you. Be right back."

THE GIFT

Martha comes back a few minutes later and sits down. In her hand, she holds an object that Dee can't quite make out. "I'm going to explain something to you about what I'm holding in my hand. First, I'm going to give you a little background on how I acquired it. You might have seen the infomercial on TV. It's called Ancestry.com. They even have resources where they can take one's DNA and see how far back someone's bloodline goes. Fortunately, the women in our family's past didn't need to do any of that.

Some of our ancestors, especially on the woman's side lived very long and had what some would call prosperous lives. Others of our family tree have been less fortunate.

I also had another daughter, your mother's sister. I had complications and she died at birth. Her name was Elizabeth. There has never been any reason for me to bring this up till now. You were only seven years old when your grandfather passed. You know my son died at an early age also.

Dee quietly says, "I am so sorry to hear about your first daughter, I didn't know. I kind of remember grandpa. Mom told me about your son that passed away while he was in a war."

Martha looked into Dee's eyes and said, "When your father died your mother never quite got over it. It was such a tragedy. He was a very good man, a loving man. He was a bit wild, adventurous in his own way. He was a believer in Christ and loved you and my daughter with all his heart. We never really get over the tragic things that happen in our lives. But for those of us that believe, we gather strength through God to go on with our lives. Not forgetting, no, never forgetting. Through Jesus Christ, we learn to let the grief subside. We put grief, sorrow, and sadness in that special place and go on with our lives.

My grandmother, your great-grandmother lived to be ninety-two years old. One never knows, when God will call us home. The key is to always be ready. That should be the main priority, foremost in all our lives.

What I am about to tell you is true. There has always been a tradition in our family dating as far back as any of us can remember.

On the 17th birthday of one's granddaughter, the girl's grandmother was bound by oath and obligated to pass on, what I can only describe as true and sacred evidence of a great symbol of faith.

I believe that the definition of ultimate truth is simply, the reality of God. There is an old saying and it goes like this, 'If you don't stand for something you will fall for anything. 'There are many among us that are weak in faith and even more that have no faith or trust in God whatsoever.

I am not trying to make it too complicated, because really, it is quite easy to understand. Dee's grandmother unfolds the cloth that she holds in her hand. Martha reaches out and hands the item, within the cloth, over to her granddaughter.

Dee takes a closer look. At first, the object looked like a dull, small angular block of aged wood. It was cracked and wrinkled, like the surface of an extremely old blackened piece of bark from an ancient oak tree. Now holding it in her hand, she sees that the material looks more like a very old dried up piece of weathered leather.

Instantly, Dee imagines she feels a mild warm sensation moving up her arm. She immediately drops it and squeaks, "Gram, sorry about that. I thought I felt something."

As she bent over to pick it back up, she mumbled, "It scared me for a sec."

Her grandmother just sits quietly observing Dee's reaction. Dee, giving it a closer look, moves it around in her hand. She sees it is leather-bound all the way around the surface of what appears to be a box, with no visible openings.

Martha whispers, "Are you okay?"

Dee replies, "I'm fine Gram. Maybe it was just a bit of electricity from the rug. What is this thing anyway?"

Not wanting to frighten her granddaughter. But on the other hand, wanting to let her know the magnitude of responsibility she was placing on her, she revealed the story of the box as was told to her many years ago.

There was a stillness throughout the room as Martha began to explain what Dee now held in her hand, represented much of her ancestry.

Over the years, many of her family's records had either been destroyed by war or other unfortunate events.

"The personal stories of our ancestors have always been told from mouth to mouth, from generation to generation. What I have just given you is a box handed down to us from antiquity.

Our first known ancestors came from Rome and Israel. They branched out into different parts of the world, spreading the word of God. What you now hold in your hand is an element of vestige. A remnant of history, that has been entrusted to the daughters of our family for centuries, to keep safe from those that would destroy it."

In a small soft-spoken voice, Dee asks, "What's in the box Gram? Is it like some bones or something?"

"No darling, you see that small little strip of leather on the very edge there? Gently pull on it."

Dee slowly starts to tug on the leather strand. The thread gradually starts to unravel. The first thing she notices is the brilliant reflection Illuminating out from the corner of the box. She continues, suddenly she shouts, "Gram, is this gold?"

She gently slips the ancient leather casing off the box. Her hands began to tremble. A feeling of great sorrow starts to emerge from within her heart. Seconds later it dissipates into a symphony of joy. Excitement and hope fill every part of her being. Martha looks at her granddaughter and remembers like it was yesterday when she herself was given the golden box.

She nods at Dee. "Go ahead darling, open it."

"Gram, I don't know if I can. My heart's beating like a scared rabbit. It's such a huge responsibility and I don't even know what is inside this box."

"Dalene, I'm not sure any of the women in our family really ever had much of a choice when we were entrusted with this. I always figured it was just expected of us to do what our hearts lead us to do. My thoughts on it are this, God has a calling for all of us. It's up to us if we want to listen for it and accept it when we hear it."

Dee carefully opens the box. Inside resting on a plush cushion of some sort of purple material, lies three oversized nails.

The three nails were tinged with what looked like a patina of dull dark discoloration, they resembled thin spikes more than nails.

Dee lets out a big sigh. "This is astonishing. Gram, how could this be? I know exactly what these are supposed to be, but? This is incredible. Who would ever believe this?"

"Sweetie, that just might be the whole point as to why our family were entrusted with them. Who would believe it? There are in this time period alone, different institutions throughout the world that are claiming to possess the crucifixion nails of Jesus Christ.

Do many people believe the Shroud of Turin is the true image of Christ? Or that the small slivers of wood, supposedly from his cross, that the Vatican covets so much, are real?

Does the Vatican really possess the true chalice that was supposedly used by Christ at the Last Supper? What about the crown of thorns? Most people are never even allowed to view any of Rome's supposed sacred relics. How many people believe in the Bible?

When compared to the world, the whole world, only a handful of us believe in our Lord and Savior Jesus Christ. With all my heart, I truly believe these are the very nails that held our Lord to the Cross."

A BIRTHDAY LIKE NO OTHER

"Gram, my head is spinning. Can we go outside for a minute? I'm feeling a little woozy. I just don't know what to think."

Dee takes the leather case and slips it back over the box. Now she carefully retreads it tight so none of the boxes surface shows.

"Ok, let's go for a little walk. We're going to check on Harold. He's always wandering around. Sometimes I can't find him. Maybe I'll put a bell around his neck. Do you think he would like that?"

Dee slips the box into her purse, and says, "Okay Gram, let's do that, let's go."

They walk out back and start to pass the old barn, Dee gestures with her hand. "What's in that old barn anyway?"

She spots a lock on it and asks, "Why do you keep it locked up?"

"Oh, I almost forgot. I think there's a little something in there for your birthday."

"Gram? You're kidding, right? Not only was I born again today but I got the shock of my life. What more could I ever want?"

"Well, it certainly isn't anything as grand as what you've experienced today though I think you might like it."

With that being said, Martha unlocks the old wooden barn doors. She swings one wide open and then the other. Dee's mouth falls open. She stares into the entrance of the small barn. It's late afternoon and the sun is just beginning to set. The last of the sun's light starts to fade but shines its rays of remaining brightness on a pure white object that sits just inside the entrance of the barn. It seemed like it was waiting silently, as if watching for Dee and her grandmother. There, like a low-slung arctic cat, ready to pounce, is a flawless pearlescent white 325i BMW.

"Gram, you're not serious. It's so beautiful! I can't take this."

"Nonsense child, Sure you can. It's not like it's new. In fact, it's twenty years old. It's older than you are. I've had this little beauty for several years. Your grandfather gave it to me. I've decided I don't need it and I wanted you to have it. I don't drive much anymore. I worked out a sweet deal with Uber and some of the local cabs around here.

Besides, now you don't have to rely on your mother all the time when you want to come and see me. She mentioned to me that you had got your learners permit and then told me later, you got your license through Drivers Ed at school last year. So, I thought this would be perfect for you."

"It's better than perfect Gram. This whole day has been like a dream even if I was a bit anxious about the box and nails. It is such a big responsibility."

Monday morning came around quickly. Dee was glad that her mom showed up early at her grandmother's house. When Dee showed her mother the car, it seemed like her mother got more excited than she did when she first saw the car.

Joanna turned to Martha and chuckled, "Mom how come I didn't know that you had kept this car around all these years. For some reason, I thought you had sold it when we were still back home."

"I guess there were a couple of things I neglected to mention to you until the time was right. You were just not to great at keeping secrets. Remember when I got the Volkswagen? That's when I put this car in storage. You, your dad and I, we all had so much fun back then, I guess I just wanted to hold on to it for the good memories. I had it shipped out here a while back. I knew that someday I was going to surprise Dee with it."

FRIENDS

Joanna pulled out her phone and quickly called her insurance company. It only took about 10 minutes to give them her daughter's information. They were off and running after both gave hugs and kisses to Martha.

Following her mother home in her new car, she felt freedom like she had never felt before. When they got home, she posted up in her room and pondered about the experience she had gone through at her grandmother's house.

Dee was also thinking, how she should break the news of the box to her mother. Apparently, she knew nothing about that either. She only had about forty-five minutes to get ready for school. She didn't have a chance to bring it up. She thought, subconsciously she wanted to hold on to her secret a little longer. Still reeling from the events of her birthday, a few days later, she still thought she felt like a different person.

The week had gone well. It was now Friday afternoon and the school had just let out. In the parking lot, while standing around her car, Dee chatted it up with a couple of her girlfriends. They were telling her about a place called Wrights Lake. They thought it was only a couple of hours from town. It would a beautiful drive. Her two friends were making plans to go up there tomorrow. It would be a lot of fun and they would love to show it to her. One of the girls, whose name was Nicole was describing the place to Dee just as two boys walked up behind them.

"Hey Dee, what's up? We saw you and your two pals over here. Just thought we'd come by and say hello."

She had changed classes early in the school year and had hardly noticed them because of the size of the campus. It had been months since she first had words with them and had all but forgotten about it.

Wanting to be polite, she goes, "You know my friends Nicole and Sarah?"

The taller one answers, "Yeah, Sarah was in my math class last semester, but we never talked much."

"I don't think I ever got your names."

"My name is Tom this is Jerry."

That sounded funny to Dee for some reason. She bit her tongue so as not to laugh. She just kind of grunts, "Well I gotta go."

"Tom keeps talking, nice wheels. We remember where you live. Maybe we can come by sometime and go for a ride."

Dee shoots back with, "Probably not."

She spins around and opens the car door, as her two friends giggle and hop in with her. Nicole asks Dee, "What was that all about? Dee shrugs, I have no idea."

Right then, Sarah says, "This is such a beautiful car it feels brand new. I was going to drive my mom's car tomorrow, but would you mind if we take yours instead?"

"No problem, I love driving this car."

Sarah adjusts her safety belt and says, "Have you named it yet?"

THE LAKE

Dee's up early Saturday morning and feeling excited about the day trip.

She's in her room getting ready when her mom passes by and peeks her head in long enough to say, "Have a beautiful day. I'm going to be gone for a while. I have a date with a friend I met at the bank. He's going to take me to a farmers market this morning, then we're going to take a drive over the hill and go to a beach in Santa Cruz. You have a great time with your friends. I'll see you around dinner time."

"Hey Mom, good luck on your outing. I'm going on a mini road trip with a couple of my girlfriends."

Her mother was already out the door and didn't even hear her.

When her friends at school had told her about Wright's Lake, they certainly hadn't been exaggerating, although it took a little over four hours to get there.

The drive up Highway 50 was breathtaking. Cruising through the park itself, was just extraordinary. A forest of redwood, birch and pine trees. Flowers blooming, birds chirping everywhere. The serenity of the lake itself, surrounded by picturesque mountains. It couldn't have been a more perfect setting.

The girls hiked, had a picnic, even swam in the pleasantly warm water. By the time they started for home, it was getting close to dusk.

Winding back out of the lake's park, while listening to their favorite CD, Dee stepped on the gas a little, after crossing over a small bridge. When she started to change the CD, it slipped out of her hand. On reflex, instead of letting Nicole get it, she reaches down between her legs and not finding it, she glances down.

THUMP! The whole car shakes. "Oh my gosh, shouts Dee, "What was that?"

Nicole sitting in the front with Dee, Sarah in the backseat, both crane their necks and stick their heads out the windows.

Nicole shouts, "No, no don't pull over. I don't want to see what you hit. Don't be crazy."

"Let's just keep on going," Sarah chirps, from the back seat.

"I know, you're not trying to get in trouble. Let's just get out of here."

Dee hesitates for a second and starts to slow down.

Sarah whines, "Hey, what are you doing?"

Nicole turns around to look at Sarah and says, "Shut up, of course, she has to stop. We don't even know what she hit."

Dee, stops the car, pulls over to the side of the road. She grabs her purse and at a fast pace starts to head back. The girls bail out of the car and run to catch up to Dee. There, lying on the side of the road is a small deer.

Sarah pulls up first. "Oh wow, you hit a deer-killed it. Your grandmother is not going to be so happy about that big dent either."

Nicole retorts with, "Sarah, can't you just for once, shut it?"

Dee quietly murmurs, "I didn't mean to do it. I never even saw it. It ran right out in front of me."

Sarah asks, "Are you sure it's even dead?"

Nicole replies, "Yeah it's dead, you don't see it moving, do you? There is nothing we can do about it. So, let's just get out of here."

Dee, looks at the girls and says, "You know what? I'm going to call 911 and report it. Someone will come and take it away."

She bends down to get a closer look at it. She fumbles around in her oversized purse, trying to find her phone, while the two other girls, looking wide-eyed, just stand there and watch.

Dee is shaking so badly that she must put her big purse down on the ground. She finally finds her phone, pulls it out of her bag. The overstuffed purse falls over and some of her things tumble out. Lipstick, a hairbrush, eyeliner, and some gum.

The small box her grandmother gave her, slides to the ground with the rest of the stuff. Dee starts to scoop it all back up. As she picks up the box, she accidentally brushes the deer's hind leg with her other hand. Out of the corner of her eye, she thinks she sees the little doe's leg twitch. Dee, grabs the box, shoves it back into her bag along with all the rest of her stuff that fell out and starts to rise back up. Suddenly, she squeaks! Jumps back, nearly losing her balance almost falling into Nicole.

Both the other girls react and quickly step back also. The small deer raises its neck up a little. Shakes its head back and forth, looks at them, then leaps to its feet, turns and in a flash, it's up and moving back into the forest of trees.

Dee stares, somewhat in shock, as the tiny animal disappears back into the foliage. "That was scary... I thought for sure I had killed it."

Nicole whispers, "Hey it was just dazed right? I mean?"

Dee thinks for a minute, had the box touched the deer's leg? She couldn't be sure. Without saying a word, she started back to the car. "Come on girls, it's going to get dark soon, we need to get back. At least my mom got me insurance."

QUESTIONS

That night while in her room, Dee lays on her bed reminiscing about the occurrence with the young doe. Earlier she has gone online and Googled some questions about the existence of the crucifixion nails of Christ and the golden box.

She could not find any reference to either of them except for a vague mention of some nails a Roman Catholic Church had acquired and a pendant shaped like nails offered for purchase on a site at https://3crucifixionnails.com.

Why she even kept the box with her, instead of putting it somewhere safe, was a question she could not answer. The box alone was probably worth hundreds of dollars if not thousands. It was about nine inches long and three inches wide. It wasn't thick but had a little weight to it. She knew it was solid.

And the little deer? What was that all about. Was I even thinking of God when that happened? Sadly, I didn't think so. Dee remembered her grandmother telling her, God has a calling for everyone.

She wondered what hers might be. Getting sleepy, Dee closes her eyes and asks the spirit of Jesus for guidance. Just before drifting off to sleep, she still couldn't imagine what God had in store for her.

COMPLICATIONS

All was going well, everything in Dee's world seemed to be a blessing. Summer was approaching and everyone was enjoying the warm breezy days. One afternoon after the last gym class, Dee walked into the locker room to change her clothes and there in the corner by the lockers, she spotted her friend Sarah sitting with Nicole. Dee notices Nicole has been crying. Sarah tells Dee that Nicole just got through with one of those mandatory school physical examinations they hold once a year.

Sarah said to Dee, the lady doctor told Nicole she had a lump under her left breast, and she was concerned about it. The doctor said it didn't feel right. It could possibly be malignant. Nicole started to sob even more.

Dee puts her hand on her friend's shoulder. "Easy girl, you don't know for sure. Don't start thinking negatively. I'll never forget when one of my mom's friends once told me, 'Do not create obstacles while assuming conflicting conditions. Meaning, don't be thinking up negative stuff just because you get worried about something. Keep a positive outlook."

Nicole tries to talk through her tears, "The doctor said, I have to go to the hospital for more tests on Monday."

Leaving school, Dee drops Sarah off at her house first. Then decides to ask Nicole to come over for a while before taking her home. When the girls arrive at the house, there is a note on the fridge that says, "I will be out for a while, fix yourself something for dinner."

After lounging around Dee's room watching videos on YouTube and listening to music for a while, Dee asks Nicole, "What church do you go to?"

Nicole spurts, "Why would you ask me that?"

"I was just wondering, I'm trying to find a church I feel comfortable with, so I thought maybe. You know, because we never really talked about anything like church before, you might know of a cool one to go to."

Nicole cuts in, "I do believe in God. It's just my parents aren't really that religious. We hardly ever go to church."

Dee heard her own inner voice saying, pretty much the same thing I would have said not so long ago.

Dee then asks, "what do you think about Jesus? Do you believe in him?" Then goes on to say, "There are hundreds if not thousands of religions in the world. It seems like all of them are reaching out and searching for God.

If one thinks about Christianity, it is the only religion and I don't even want to call it that, where God reaches out to you. You see, the reason I'm not trying to bother calling Christianity religion is that when you accept Christ into your life, this becomes a personal relationship with him, an intimate relationship.

My grandmother was right when she told me, going to church all the time, reading the Bible three or four times a day, thinking you're a good person by being kind and helping others. that is all wonderful. But the bottom line is, as believers in Jesus, we should be doing that anyway.

Why? You might ask, for the gratification and thanks, praise and glory for what Jesus has done for us. He died on the cross to wash us of our sins. There is no way we could ever have done it by ourselves."

Nicole just sat there and listened, didn't interrupt. She sat and thought about what Dee was saying.

“True Christians not only recognize but also understand and believe Jesus was the one who had to die by shedding his blood in order to have our sins forgiven. But also, by being resurrected on the third day, that all who believe in him, would know that he is real and not some legend, myth or made-up story. That means everything. If there had not been the supernatural occurrence of his resurrection... There would be no Christianity.”

HEALING

Nicole is taken aback, as she looks deep into Dee's eyes, she realizes she is seeing a whole new person. "You know exactly what you're talking about, don't you? You're right, I would like to learn more about Jesus."

Dee nods at her friend. "Yeah, but until recently I didn't know much about any of this. I didn't know any more than you do. I've been studying the Bible at night. It seems like my whole world is changing. What the Bible says about the word of God when someone becomes a true believer, they have the authority in Jesus Christ, to heal.

That doesn't just mean physically, it also means, emotionally, mentally and spiritually. We can help others get through hard times if we share the word of God with them."

Nicole brightens up a bit, "Like the disciples that followed him, right? Wow! How cool would that be to help people understand what Jesus is really like? How much faith would one need to have power like that to heal?"

Dee explains, "Of course, it is about faith. It is also about love, repentance, which means having a change of heart. It is accepting Jesus as your Lord and Savior. You must reach into your heart and believe with your whole being that Jesus is real.

This is no joke. It's not something to kid about. Take it from me. I will tell you the truth. The Bible is not a fairytale. It is not a book of fiction. It is even found in the nonfiction section of some regular bookstores and that's something, considering how twisted this world's getting these days.

Listen, Nicole, do you want to have a special relationship with Jesus? Do you want to get to know him intimately? All you need to do is open your heart and you will learn to love Him.

That's one of the easiest things on earth to do. At the same time, one of the hardest things to do in this world is to be sincere and maintain that relationship through the rest of your life. Nicole, I want to pray for you. I want to pray with you. I want to pray about your problem. Can I do that for you? I mean, can we pray right now?"

"Yes, Dee, I would really like that. I don't know if anyone has ever prayed for me before. And I am pretty sure I have never prayed with someone before."

Dee has thought as she pulls Nicole closer to her so they can hold hands while they pray. She reaches over to her nightstand and opens a drawer and takes out the box. She hands the small box to Nicole.

Dee, what is this? It looks like a shriveled up old frog skin. Is it a block of petrified wood or something?"

Dee laughs. "It's just an old keepsake. Been in the family forever." Nicole looks at it and says, "Whatever." She hands it back.

Dee lays the box back down in the drawer and says, "Now close your eyes and think of Jesus only. Think of how you would like to get to know him personally. Let us pray. Our Father Who Art in Heaven…"

After leading Nicole to Christ and then giving her a ride home, she wonders about this night. It was kind of strange because right in the middle of prayer, Nicole popped her eyes open and exclaimed in a low pitched voice, "I'm sorry but that was so weird, for a second I was kneeling in the rain with these other women and we were all looking up at Jesus who was hanging on a cross. I couldn't really make out his face because everything was so bright, but I knew it was him. It was all in a flash. Does that make any sense?"

Later that night, Dee, lying in her bed just shakes her head and quietly asks out loud, "God, did you want me to pray for my friend? Because it sure felt like it."

Monday at school, Dee, ran into Sarah in the hallway and asked if she has seen Nicole?

Sarah replied, "Nicole had to go to the hospital to get that check-up. When she didn't show up for school, I tried to call her, but her phone was off. I just hope she is okay. I'll try to call her in a couple of hours, you try to call her also."

Later that afternoon, Dee, pulled up to her house and saw Nicole, standing out in front talking with her mother. Before she's even halfway out of her car, Nicole comes bounding down the driveway with a big tooth-paste commercial smile on her face.

"Dee, I can't believe it girl, I'm okay. All the tests came back negative." Nicole laughs. "It was a fat deposit and the doctor said, 'It should dissolve itself in time.' I'm so thankful for you. I really believe our prayers had a lot to do with it. I have been praying thanks to Jesus all morning. I was just telling your mom how you prayed for me, how we prayed together."

Joanna interrupts them. "Do I have a healer in the family?"

Dee responds, "Mom quit kidding around. This was serious. Nicole was really scared but she's okay now. That's all that matters."

Joanna counters, "Your grandmother had a knack for stuff like that. She never liked to talk about it, but I remember finding a little bird on the ground and she–"

"Mom! It was nothing like that, we just prayed is all."

Dee ended up giving Nicole a ride home. She decided she would say something about the box the next time she saw her mom.

The following morning as Dee came out of the bathroom, she saw her mom down the hallway. "Hey mom, if you got a minute there's something, I wanted to talk to you about."

Joanna answers, "Of course, sweetie. Can it wait till later? I have a big date, a very important date, and I'm already late."

Dee shrugs, "Sure mom it can wait, have a great time."

That night sitting on the couch after watching a bunch of nothing on television. She gets up, turns it off and goes into her bedroom. She grabs her Bible and takes it back out into the living room with her.

She knows Christs' crucifixion was written about in the New Testament. She starts reading the Gospel of John. A quarter of the way through, she flashes on the fact that Nicole didn't mention anything about holding the box just before they prayed. Guess that was a good thing, as she would have had some explaining to do.

Sometime later, she came to the part about the three Mary's and realized they were not only at Jesus' crucifixion but were also with him when he was laid to rest. She lays the Bible down, thinks about Nicole's vision for just a minute, then thanks Jesus for coming into her life and drifts off into a peaceful sleep.

THE TRIP

Three more weeks before school is out for the summer, Joanna had received a bonus and was feeling bad for not spending more time with her daughter. She thinks it would be fun to do something together over the weekend.

Thursday morning, while sitting together at the breakfast table, Joanna asks Dee, if perhaps she might like to take a little road trip and hang out at Lake Tahoe for a couple of days. Perhaps see a show or two.

Dee gives her mom a big smile. She says, "She'd like that a lot but only if they could go to a church together on Sunday while they were up there."

Joanna looked a bit surprised, "Sure Hun, whatever you'd like to do."

They started out early Saturday morning, not in a hurry to get to the summit. As they topped the mountain, they beheld the beauty of the lake. The view from above Lake Tahoe was breathtaking. Like a gigantic sapphire set in the middle of an emerald forest green. They drove down the mountain and checked into an upscale resort right on highway 50 called The Lodge. Not wanting to waste any time, they looked through a couple of brochures that were set up near the reception area. They both decided to take a cruise that included lunch. It sounded exciting as it would be on a paddlewheel boat called the Tahoe Queen.

After a spectacular afternoon, Dee and her mother went back to the Lodge to freshen up. Later, that evening they ended up having a beautifully prepared buffet at Harrah's. Then decided to take a walk around the casino, stopping so Dee could watch her mom play a couple of dollar slots, even though Dee, not being of age, was the one who slipped the dollars in the machines.

It was now time to head over to Harveys Cabaret and watch two famous comedians who were featured at The Improv.

Early Sunday morning they were up early, checked out of the Lodge and drove around to the other side of the lake, where they stopped and had a delightful meal of Norwegian style blueberry pancakes at a small breakfast nook called the Log Cabin Cafe in Kings Beach. They found a quaint little chapel named the North Shore Church of Hope and enjoyed a wonderful service there together. Then they decided to head back home, each one content in her own thoughts knowing the outing couldn't have been better.

TROUBLE

Joanna and Dee got into town a few hours later. as they drove down their street, they could see the flashing lights of two police cruisers parked in their driveway. Joanna jumps out of the car door with the quickness. She passes by a couple of gawking neighbors and shouts to an officer.

"Excuse me, sir, excuse me! This is my home. We live here. What's happening?" Just then, another officer rounds the side of the house.

He hears Joanna and replies, "Hi there, I'm Sergeant McCleod of the San Jose police department. We received a call, apparently, a couple of kids broke into your house. One of your neighbors saw them go around back and called 911. Luckily, we had a car in the area. When the officer flipped on the siren your neighbor heard it.

The kids must have also heard it, because your neighbor said, 'They dashed out the front door a few seconds later.'

He lives across the street and told us he could possibly ID them but he wasn't wearing his glasses so he might not be sure."

The officer continued, "Do you mind if we can all go into the house. Perhaps you can take an inventory to see if anything is missing."

Joanna leads the officers into the house. Things looked a bit out of order. Some items were piled on the dining room table, but nothing seemed to be missing.

Dee, in the meantime, rushed to her bedroom. It was a mess. The drawers were open, clothes were scattered on the floor. Drawers were half pulled out and the closet door was open. She looked around. She didn't see her laptop; it was nowhere to be seen.

Her tablet and an old iPad were missing also. Then she noticed her nightstand drawer was opened. She thought, please no but yes, the box was gone. She folded unto the floor, devastated. Who could she even tell? Her mom didn't even know about it. The only one that knew about the golden box and the three nails was her grandmother. Through her tears, she starts to fume, making herself more upset each moment she thought about it. Mad at herself for even accepting the box as a gift.

She takes in a few deep breaths, wipes her eyes, tries to shake everything off and goes back into the living room. The officer says he's sorry about this. He tells them that they need to make an inventory of things that are missing. A few minutes later, Dee starts on the list and doesn't even bother listing the box. Like who would ever believe her anyway.

After the police left, Dee's mom tells her not to worry. "Everything can be replaced."

Little did her mom know. Dee went to her room, shut the door, sat on her bed and cried. That night she prayed. She asked Jesus to accept her repentance for anything she had done to displease God. She asked the Holy Spirit to please guide her for she didn't know what to do about losing the nails.

Dee didn't go to school on Monday or Tuesday. She decided to go and see her grandmother. She had tried to call but just got a voicemail. She left a message letting her know she was going to come to see her the next day.

PANIC

It was about 10:30 in the morning by the time Dee pulled up to her grandmother's house. For some reason, it felt curiously quiet. She hopped out of her car and went to the front door. On the fourth knock, just when she started to suspect no one is home, Lauren, one of Martha's housemates answered the door.

"Hi Dee, I didn't have your cell number. I tried to call your mom last night, but I couldn't get through. Your grandmother was at the mall with her friend from church when she had some kind of stroke."

"Dee freezes and then says, "Where is she?"

"They took her to El Camino hospital In Los Gatos, it was the closest."

Dee was already running back to her car. God, what is happening? Why now? Please let her be okay.

She powers out of the driveway and GPS's the name of the hospital. She steers the car with one hand and while holding her phone in the other hand, asking Google to connect her to her mom. When she hears her mom's voice on the other end of the phone she blurts out, "Mom? Grams in the hospital. I'm on my way I can meet you there."

"Johanna moans, Dee, I'm in San Francisco, in the middle of a meeting. I'll get out of this and be there asap. Text me the info, I'll text you when I'm on my way."

Dee makes it to the hospital in record time. She goes to the front desk and inquires as to where her grandmother is. She quietly enters the room and sees her grandmother lying in an oversized bed. She looks fragile and tired.

Her eyes are closed but when she hears Dee enter, she blinks, opens her eyes and looks directly at her.

"Oh Gram, I'm so sorry if I had only known."

Martha retorts, "Known what? I didn't even know. One minute everything is just dandy, the next minute I'm on my butt. Very embarrassing. They say it could have been a mild stroke. Which means until they run me through a gauntlet of tests they don't even know, besides not being able to move my left arm so well and that's because I think I hit it on a chair when I fell, I feel fine."

As her grandmother was speaking, Dee's mind was going a mile a minute. She felt that somehow if she hadn't lost the box and had brought it with her, it could help her grandmother.

She wanted to say something about it but thought if she told her what happened, she might make things worse.

"Gram let me pray for you. I'm so scared for you. I don't know what I'd do if something happened to you. Like if you–"

Martha interrupts. "Child, I don't need you to pray for me. I have had a wonderful life. If God is calling me? If he wants me? So be it. I give all praise and glory to him. I have been ready to go home for a while now. Dalene, trust me, I am tired. I want to see my husband Zach, my son John and be with my daughter. There are so many more people I know, that are with the Lord and to tell you the truth, I can't wait to be with them. So, my darling, I want you to pray with me, not for me."

Dee takes hold of her grandmother's hand. "Gram, if only I had brought the box. I know it would have helped."

Martha looks at her granddaughter and shakes her head. "Now that the nails and box are in your care, please, let's not get this twisted. Those three nails are a true symbol of Christ's existence. As is the gospel of Jesus' disciples, and the whole Bible for that matter. The only supernatural power I will ever believe in is the power given to true believers, through our Lord and Savior Jesus Christ.

This is all the power, hope and faith one will ever need to get through this life. Keep your spiritual eyes and ears open. Encase yourself in the armor of God, as those nails are encased in the golden box.

God will always know what is on the inside. How about we say a prayer of thanks that we each are allowed even one more day."

A moment after prayer, Dee's phone rings. It is her mom letting her know she is on her way. Martha asks Dee, to come back and to see her tomorrow afternoon. "Now go home and get some rest."

CONSEQUENCES

Dee drove home from the hospital in an angry state. In a flash, she had figured out why she was so mad. Out of nowhere, she had felt a growing suspicion of who had broken into her house.

Pulling up to her house, she noticed someone on the front steps. As she got out of her car and started to walk up the driveway, she could barely believe her eyes. She had an epiphany about the break-in. Now it was like she had conjured him up out of thin air. She kept walking forward.

The young man stood up and said, "I've been waiting for you."

In front of her stood Jerry. One of the boys that had harassed her a few different times. For a moment all Dee could see was red.

Jerry raises his hands up says, "I know, I know." He put his hands back down.

"I know you must be thinking that I'm like the biggest jerk ever. I came to apologize. To say, I'm really sorry for breaking into your house. It was totally stupid of me for listening to Tom."

He continues, "Look, it's all here."

As he starts to open his backpack, he keeps talking. "All your stuff is in here. I brought back everything that Tom also took, I swear. I told him I was an idiot and I was going to turn myself in. I don't think he believed me." Jerry starts putting things down on the porch.

Dee looks it over and asks, "Jerry, where's the box?"

He gets a startled look on his face. "We never took any box."

Dee's all, "Yeah right. The little box that was in my nightstand."

"Oh, you mean that thing. The thing that looked like an old block of wood? You had it stuck way in the back of your nightstand? What was that anyway?

I grabbed it thinking it was an old piece of petrified wood or something and I think it burnt me. That little thing felt hot. I threw it down and kicked it out of the way I wouldn't have picked it up again on a bet. My hand stayed red for two days."

Dee growls, "You better not move. Just stay here for a minute I'll be right back."

She turns, opens the front door and raced to her room, falls on her hands and knees and starts looking under her bed. Finding nothing she scoots over to her nightstand. She puts her face to the rug so she can see under the bed and starts looking around.

There in the farthest corner, practically hidden out of sight, way back under her nightstand is the box. Dee comes back outside and starts to gather up her things.

Jerry says, "Do you believe me? I'm not that guy anymore. Please don't be angry with me, I am truly sorry. I have been trying to see you for a couple of days now. I'm not sure what came over me. But when I got home that night, I felt very strange.

You probably won't believe me but when I was in my room, I heard a small soft-spoken voice, not telling me but asking me to change my ways. It was like a whisper, I had no idea where it was coming from but I couldn't sleep a wink that night, I asked God for forgiveness. Not just for what I did that day at your place but for everything.

I'm not going to blame anything on Tom. It was my decision to go with him. Whatever the consequences of this, from now on, I'm going to be my own person and think for myself with the help of God. Right now, I'm also asking for your forgiveness. I'm truly sorry."

"Jerry, just get out of here. I don't want my mom to see you when she gets home. But hey! Thanks for owning up to it and bringing my stuff back.

Oh, and Jerry, I do forgive you but what is much more important is for you to realize, Jesus has forgiven you. You're on the right track, no matter what happens. Right now, is the perfect time to change your life. Let God be your guide from now on."

Dee walks back into the house. Goes straight to her room picks up the box off her bed and while holding it tight in both hands she kneels and with tears of joy, goes into the fetal position, thanking God repeatedly.

TRUST IN GOD

Dee's mother finally arrived back from the hospital around 8:30 that night. Right when she walked through the front door, Dee asked her how her grandmother was doing?

Joanna shook her head. "I'm not really sure. When I was there, she seemed like her normal self. She said she had a little pain in her left arm and that was about it. The doctors were still running tests, visiting hours were over, I left she could get some sleep.

Dee, both of us have had a long day, so let's call it a night. Try and get a good night's rest, I love you."

9:00 the next morning Dee was up and out of the door. Shouting out behind her that she was off to see her grandmother, "She told me not to go to see her until this afternoon but I'm going now. I'll text you and let you know what's up."

It was closer to 10:00 in the morning, because of the morning traffic by the time she got to the hospital.

She walked in and not seeing anybody posted up at the nurse's station, she bypassed the front desk and kept on walking. She proceeded on to her grandmother's room.

As she enters the room, she immediately saw that the bed was empty. Her eyes caught a bit of movement to the left and she spotted an orderly cleaning up the restroom.

Dee blurts out. “Excuse me, pardon me? Do you know where my grandmother is?

The orderly, an older Filipino man looked down shook his head and said, “I came on about one hour ago. Your grandmother is gone. I am sorry. The nurse told me to clean up.”

Dee cries, "Oh, no. She drops the flowers she had brought and the little box in her other hand started to feel like a heavy piece of lead. She felt dizzy so she sat down on a chair. Finished with the restroom the orderly quietly slipped past her. Dee began to weep.

"God, is this the way things work? Just in a blink of an eye and the world as we know it disappears? I would have liked to have said goodbye."

It seemed like forever, but it was probably only a few minutes later when a nurse walks by and sees Dee sitting on the chair crying.

"Hi there, young lady. What's going on here? Are you okay?"

Teary-eyed, Dee looks up at the nurse. "My grandmother passed away this morning. I was too late; I know I could have helped her. She passed away before I got here. I'm just really sad."

The nurse tilts her head thinking a moment. "The elderly lady that was in this room? What was her name?

Dee could hardly answer. Through her sniffles, she sighs, "Her name was Martha. Martha De'Angelo."

The nurse tells Dee not to move. "Just sit tight for a minute." She said, "I need to check on something."

Not even five minutes later the nurse returns to the room carrying a clipboard and has a big grin on her face. Dee is perplexed. The nurse smiles and informs her, "Your grandmother did not die here today. I was told that things weren't as bad as the doctors had feared. It seems your grandmother had a bad case of indigestion, cramping, on top of having a very severe acid reflux reaction. The doctor's report said, your grandmother's body reacted to something she ate, and her arm was bruised from the fall."

Dee was speechless for a moment. She could barely whisper, "Thank you."

Dee literally ran out of the hospital and jumped into her car. She gave herself about a couple of minutes to control her breathing and then tried to call her mother. No answer. She texted her. "Gram is okay and back home. I'm going there now."

Dee parked her car and ran up the steps just as the other one of her grandmother's housemates opened the front door.

"Come on in you must be Dalene, oops, I mean Dee. I'm Bethany. It's so nice to finally meet you. Martha always speaks very highly of you. She is in her room resting but I think she knew you would be coming by soon. I'm pretty sure she is awake."

Dee replies, "it was very nice to meet you too."

She side-steps her and enters the house. Coming into her grandmother's room and seeing her standing by the window, gazing out at a small apple orchard she quietly says, "Gram? Shouldn't you be in bed?"

"Come and sit with me. Remember when you came to the hospital? Of course, I do. Yes, but remember when you wanted to pray for me, and I told you to save it? I said let's pray together. Well, my dear, I was thinking you didn't hear me very well. You went ahead and silently prayed for me to get better anyway, didn't you? And I just remembered, as you were praying, you held my arm."

Dee shyly answers, "Why would you think that? And besides, I love you, Gram. How could I not pray for you?"

"Dalene, then when we were holding hands finishing up with prayer just before your mom called, I got a very warm sensation in both my arms. Child, I felt that same feeling a long time ago. I fell off my bicycle. I thought for sure something was broken. My grandmother helped me off the ground. I started feeling that same warmth all over. I also started to feel better immediately. I didn't think much of it until later in life. I saw the effect that my grandmother had on other people. Why do you think I was up and out of the hospital so early this morning?

When I woke up my arm felt completely fine. Like it had never been hurt in the first place. Even the doctors were a little amazed. No box, no nails. It was just you, me and Jesus in the room."

Dee just sat there listening not knowing what to say. Then in a whisper, "Gram? What are you trying to say?"

Her grandmother continues talking. "Dee, trust me when I say to you God has big plans for you. Look at all the madness that is going on around us. The so-called natural disasters, the mass killings, a lot of those massacres were done by children.

There is a multitude of people denying their own gender. Others condoning gay and lesbian rights. Sweetheart, always remember not to judge and never hate the sinner, hate the sin, for we all fall short of the glory of God.

Still, it's all so disheartening, this world is changing so fast and not for the better. Even the abortion laws keep changing for one state to the next. Right now, it's pro-life in very few states and legalized abortion in almost all the other states.

"There are regular everyday people that seem quite normal one minute then flipping the switch and going nuts the next minute. Some are on drugs and alcohol, some not. They are not only harming themselves but are harming others also. At some point very soon I'm going to talk to you about spiritual warfare. Believe me I would never even bring up that subject if at wasn't so important. And Don't even get me started on the huge opiate drug epidemic that is literally killing thousands of Americans. And if that isn't enough, read what that Swedish girl Grata Thunburg, who is the same age as you, has to say about the global climate The world is in big trouble and God is not only very sad about it...He is very angry.

At this very moment, as He has done all through time, He is choosing ambassadors, warriors, instructors and counselors to represent him in this world. Equipping them with special gifts to help guide the lost and bring believers home when they are ready."

"There have always been those that need to be saved and there are those that cry out to be saved. Dee, I am a big fan of acronyms and one is the initials B.R.O. meaning Belief, Repentance, Obedience. As believers, we must also be guides of light that can lead others to the truth of the gospel. I truly believe you are one of the chosen.

Dalene, I know you have been reading the Bible. You said you read the Gospel of John. Do you remember what women were not only witnesses to Jesus' crucifixion but helped lay him to rest? And who was the first to know of his resurrection?"

Dee thinks for a moment. "Yes, it was Jesus' mother Mary and one other Mary. The one that was married to Clopas. I think he was a steward to one of the royal houses. And the third one was Mary Magdal–Oh my gosh! Magdalene."

Dee had a stunned look on her face as she said, "My name is part of her name? Gram, what does that mean?

Her grandmother replies, "Who can really know our ancient heritage.

I will tell you this. Like everything else, unbelievers try to twist biblical truth and with much success, I might add. One of the things they did was to desecrate the name of Mary Magdalene. At no time in the Bible does it ever say that Mary Magdalene was a harlot or prostitute. It is said that Jesus cast out seven evil spirits that had plagued her and she was one of his most faithful followers from that moment on.

Our family dates to the 1300s. One thing is certain, someone and maybe more than one person in our family, existed in biblical times, Living in Jerusalem at the time of Christ.

Whatever God has in store for you? Please embrace it. Maybe one of the reasons I wasn't allowed to go home yet is to walk a bit more with you on your new path."

"Gram! I have no idea what that path can possibly be. I am only 17. I have never even had a boyfriend yet. First, you entrust me with a huge responsibility of the box and nails and now you say God has some kind of mission for me? What kind of life will I have now?"

Martha solemnly answers, "I have no idea where your new journey in life will lead you. You can bet it's not always going to be pleasant. It's not always going to be easy. But please believe this, God will be by your side throughout the best of times and the worst. His angels will surround you. The Holy Spirit will guide you.

Trust in Jesus Christ and your time on earth will be a constant adventure. Your life in heaven will be glorious. Keep the golden box safe. The three nails of Christ are a memoir. The power and the authority that God has given you is through his Son Jesus and not the nails of his crucifixion. Put them away and keep them protected with affection as you would your most precious keepsake. A treasure to pass down to your own granddaughter.

Now let us be cheerful and have a grand day and just be thankful that God has called upon us and that we have heard him."

"Gram, all this talk is making my head spin and you're going to need to get some rest now. I must be going home. I have a lot of thinking to do. I have a lot of praying to do.

One of the first things on my new agenda is to sit down and have a long talk with your daughter, my mom.

I have a very interesting story to tell her not only about our secret, I want my mother and lot of people that I haven't even met yet, to know how to receive Jesus and get to heaven when the time comes. They need to learn that death is not the end but the beginning of eternal life that will either be spent in heaven or in hell. I need to tell everyone that chooses to listen to me, the good news of Jesus Christ. Even if I have to share God's word with all of them... one person at a time."

In memory of
Rachel Joy Scott
20th-century American martyr

Author's suggestion

under the Influence of Jesus Christ

Repent...
Trust and Believe